Devil's Daughter

Dark Ice

WRITERS REPUBLIC L.L.C.
515 Summit Ave. Unit R1
Union City, NJ 07087, USA

Website: *www.writersrepublic.com*
Hotline: *1-877-656-6838*
Email: *info@writersrepublic.com*

Ordering Information:
Quantity sales. Special discounts are available on quantity purchases by corporations, associations, and others. For details, contact the publisher at the address above.

Library of Congress Control Number: 2021937554
ISBN-13: 978-1-63728-335-6 [Paperback Edition]
978-1-63728-336-3 [Digital Edition]

Rev. date: 04/23/2021

Contents

I would like to dedicate this book to my older sister Chrissy.
If it was not for her I would not have started writing.

CHAPTER ONE
The dark tale

"Widows shook as the wind hit the widow's pain. There is a short breath under the bed, as a young girl hides under it. The creeks from the floorboards start coming towards the closed lock doors, footsteps stop, and the door handle riddles with great force. It stops and all goes quiet. The little girl thinks she is safe and crawls from underneath the bed. She walks towards the window and looks out, thinking the coast is clear she turns around. From the outside you could hear her blood-curdling scream from two miles away," the village story told. All the kids around him scooted closer towards him. They all were in awe, with their mouths wide open, and their eyes glitter with excitement. All except one, a twelve-year-old girl called Adieu Aloe. She was entrusted with mysteries that made sense and had a fantastic ending. Unlike the rest of the people in that town.

However she was a mystery kid herself, she had three holes on the side of her neck; she had them since she was five years old. Most people would think it was caused by a blood-sucking vampire, except she was still alive and was not fazed by the light and crosses. No one really knows how she got them however a few people say she got them in the Wagon crash that killed her parents. However, she has not made that her life and acts like nothing happened and everything was normal. "Sir, what happened to her? I mean who was in her house, and did she die, did she live. I need more stuff than that." she asked with an attitude. "I am sorry but that is for another day," the storyteller said with a smile. Adieu was annoyed, for that day would never come. For the village, the storyteller would go to a different story on the night before Halloween.

The nine o'clock bells rang and everyone went inside except for Adieu. For some reason, it's been like this ever since her parents died. She would be left alone to defend herself at night. It was like she was a demon of some sort for some reason every time at night for no one will be around her then. However, that day, she was like an angel. She could never understand why everyone was like that towards her. Adieu looked around and as normal it was a ghost town. Walking through the road of darkness, she creeps through the valley of loneliness once more to her lair of despair. Crawling underneath the sheets of ripped skin of her innocent victims. Vanes burns with the demons of sorrow and no exceptions, and her life burden with failure of love, and gratitude.

Eyes turn yellow with confusion, and doubt of her existence. She yarns' for a chance for the life that she once had when she was five. She would then close her eyes to the darkness of hell where she belongs. Clouds cover the night sky, drops of poison fall from heaven, like knives amid to kill any victim that gets' in the way. Death blows through the town heavily to strike down the weak. Rattling the windows as it laughs at them and time goes still as the child opens her eyes, the sky roars to welcome her back to nightlife. She found a black shadow at the end of her bed. The girl then sits up to calm her home back. The shadow moves but does not leave. "It's an alright young one, I will not hurt you." explained the shadow. "I just want out of the rain" it continued telling her.

The child lies back down in her makeshift bed but does not close her eyes. She watched the dark character that was sitting and staring out into the cold eyes of the dark. The yells of the cold winds voice that rampaged through the broken wall of defeat sent shivers down the girl's head to toe with fright. The shadow shields her from the frosty winds of death and drapes a woven cloak of pain which gives her the warmth from the fires from hell. "It is all right, I am not going to allow these demons to get a hold of you." the shadowy figure told her. The girl sets up and looks at the shadow closely, the shadow becomes a man of darkness. He was dressed in black and wore a long wavy cloak. She looks down and sees a metal rod on his side. "Who are you?" she asked a little frightened, though the man did not answer her "Here they come," the Shadow figure announced and then turned to face her.

"I am going to ask you not to be afraid of as best as you can. These demons feed on fear from everyone and everything around them. I know what I am asking is insane but you need to trust me," the strange man told her. The girl looked to see what the man was talking about and then she saw them. They were grey men with bright crimson blood-red eyes glowing. They were walking into her town. With their fangs showing, their laughs sounded like silent screams of victims in the cold night feast. Their nails were sharp like broken glass from a murderer and bloody like a newborn baby's throat had been slit. She slowly takes the potato sack off of her, these horrifying characters come closer.

"What are they," the girl asked the shadowed man. "They are demons from beyond the fires of hell, lost souls that can't find their way back." said the man. "What do they want?" asked the girl as she scooted across towards the man. "Sir why are they here?" the girl asked with entrusting. The man took his eyes off the beasts and turned to the girl. "They are looking for their victim, and until they find it they will scurry around the world looking for It." said the man. The girl's head turned back to where the beasts were. However they were gone, the man moved from where he stood. "Damn it, they're gone," he yelled out. "Sir, who are you?" the girl asked again. This time the man turned to face her, the girl did not know what he would do, however, she stood her ground. "My name is no concern to you at this moment." The man turned once more and started walking farther into the village, the girl walked back into her little shack and climbed back into her potato sack but did not fall asleep.

CHAPTER TWO
Manhunt

She was too busy thinking about the shadow man, and the beasts called demons. She closed her eyes and pried. "God, please keep your people safe, and if you are willing please allow me to find that man in the morning. I would like to ask you more questions. Thank you, Lord, for being my only friend. Amen." Once more she opened her eyes and then closed them again. Deep in the night, the shadows crept around and smugly covered the ground. Something is censorial as they walk. They reach the house and enter. They crept up the steps and came to a small white door. There was no sound, a tiny girl crawled out from under the bed; they watched her walk to the window.

They glide towards her, as she turns around she screams, as they devoured her, afterward all that was left of her was her skull and two arm bones. The blood-curdling scream traveled through the whole town. Her mother and father rush to the door "Rachel is everything okay? What's going on?" they asked as they opened the door. When they found that she was not in her bed, they first thought she was under her bed. Her parents walked towards the bed. Her father checked under the bed. A terrifying scream came from his wife, in a panic the husband hit his head on the bottom of the bed. He saw his wife's pale face, she was pointing at the window.

The day had come and it was dark with the blood, the tears of the woman who lost the will to live. The sun has hidden itself from the world. The town was crawling with people, but they all were going one way the girl got up from her boxed home; she walked towards Townsquare. *I wonder what is going on.* Adieu thought to herself. She spotted a man dressed in black, she ran up to him. "Excuse me, sir?" she started to say. The tall man in black stopped and turned towards her. She noticed that he was no one from this town. For he was dressed fully in black and had a mask over his face. But that did not stop her. "Excuse me sir but can you tell me what is going on?" she asked.

The man looked at the girl dressed in rags. "A girl has been murdered in this town," he answered. He turned away and started walking. She decided to join the party, once she got to the medal of the squire she could hear the mayor shouting. "My people of Babylon!" he spoke. "At twelve o'clock last night. The devil came and took my only child," he told everyone. Adieu could not see what was going on, so she pushed herself to the very front of the crowd. There she saw the mayor dump the remaining parts of his daughter on the dusty ground.

Everyone gasped in horror. A few of the women fainted. Adieu's only thought was that hell finally found them. Her legs went weak and she fell onto her hands and knees. Her stomach started to go in knots. The only thought that went through her head was what could have done that, could it be the demons she saw last night. No, it couldn't have been for there would be scratches on these bones, and there would be more than bones. "I will pay twenty gold pieces to the person that catches the menace that did this to my daughter." the mayor yelled.

After the whole speech from the mayor, everyone started to leave, the only one that stayed was the girl. All she could do was look at the bones in front of her. She knew by looking at them, this was not the end of the death in her village. The black clothing man went to the blacksmiths, "I need two cases of silver bullets and a gold cross." the man asked for. The young blacksmith wrote down the order, "That will be twenty-five gold pieces," the young blacksmith told him. "I need them by the end of the day, can you do that?" the man asked the boy. The boy nodded his head. In that term, the masked man went to the bar. On his way he saw that the girl had not moved, "Weak, ones that can't handle it should never look have to look upon the darkness" the masked man said to himself. The man walked into the bar and ordered himself a few whiskeys, He donned his cup when the bartender came his way.

"Who is the victim?" he asked. "Sir, the victim was Ms. Rachel. She was the only child of the mayor himself. It must have been a real shock to both him and his wife to find their daughter like that." the bartender told him. After paying the bill he asked if there was a room he could wash up in and rest. "There is one but that is a suit, I don't think you would have enough to stay in it." the bartender told him "how much?" the man asked. "Will it be about sixty gold" with that the man pulled out a sack and counted sixty gold coins, gave them to the bartender, and grabbed the key. The suite was across the dirt road from the bar, so he went outside and walked to the suit. But before he went in, he looked up the street and the girl was still on her knees, however, no one went near her.

Every time someone had to cross her path they stepped farther to the side they were on. It was like they would catch the black plague if they went near her. The man shook his head and went in and found that there was a bed, an oak disk, and a bathtub. He sat down at the disk chair when there was a knock on the door. "Who is it?" he called. "The maid. I was told to bring you bath garments," said a woman's voice. He told her to come in, and be quick with her work. When she filled up the tub with hot water, he asked her about the girl on the road. Her answer was, "she is called the cures child, and she lost her parents in a wagon incident. If you ask me she's better enough dead," the woman said. "Why would you say that?" the man asked her. "Will it's because no one wants her, only because she has the devil's mark on her," she said. "What mark is that ma'am?" he asked though the woman did not say. "It is forbidden to talk about it Sir, I just advise you to just stay away from her," the woman told him and with that she finished her work and then left.

The Man's interest was peaked from the fear and the woman's warnings that he took it upon himself to investigate. He took a decorative basin and dish from the desk and filled it. He quickly washed himself up and dressed in clean clothes. He then took out a long black shirt and placed it onto the chair and then slid his bag under the bed. The man then walked out and still saw the girl on her knees and not moving as if she was dead. "It's a pity that it wasn't that girl, poor Rachel did not deserve to die." he heard a woman whisper to another. "What do you expect from a child whose death himself evades," the other woman laughed out. "What's a pity is that a young girl is getting such treatment from those of the land of Babylon," the man scolded them as he walked away as they started hissing as if he threw holy water on them. He walked a few buildings while carefully keeping his eye on this girl in rages getting dirt kicked in her face by kids. "Excuse me, can you point me to the black smith?" the man asked the sheriff. "Yes, it's just three buildings up," the sheriff told him. "Thank you and may god bless you," the man told him and continued walking and he heard the sheriff yelling at the kids to leave the devil child alone while laughing.

He got to the Black smiths and saw a medium boy working very hard. "Son, is your father or master around?" he asked the boy. "No sir, my master is at the Mayors today fixing his house. May I ask what you have ordered and I can do the transaction with you?" the boy asked him which made the man smile. "Son, I just arrived in this town. I have no orders yet, though by the way you work I believe you can get them done for me before tomorrow." the man told him. "Will sir what would you like?" the young boy asked. "I need this silver cross fixed and a dozen silver bullets made." the man told him. "I should have that done by this evening sir." the young man told him. "Good oh and on the bottom of that cross please etch a crescent moon." the man asked the boy before leaving with the boy calling out his name to him.

The man stepped out of the blacksmith's shop and noticed the town had become a ghost town except the girl still on the ground. "Bloody hell, what is wrong with this town?" he asked himself while walking up to the girl and picking her up and taking her to his room. To his surprise this girl made no sound and did not even struggle. Once they entered the room he placed her carefully on the ground and all she did was stare at him confused. He then bent down to his knees and cuffed his hands around her face. "I need you to get undressed, go into that tub and yourself up, dress yourself in that shirt on the chair and then crawl into that bed before I get back. Do you understand?" he asked her. At first she did or said nothing and just stared, "Come on kid show me you understand what I am saying." he told her. He turned around as she got undressed and interred the tub and with that he took the torn up clothing off the ground so he could take it and have them burned.

CHAPTER THREE
In Heaven or Hell?

With a quick smile that faded before he walked out the door, and asked one of the people where he could find a clothing store. An old woman pointed to the left, and He said thank you and headed out. He came to a halt when he realized he did not know her size. Thankfully he brought her clothing so they could be burned. "ma'am" he called the women. "Yes sir?" she asked. "I need some clothing for my girl, she is a size seven. However, I need boy clothes for her. Black if you have them, it's for night hunting." he informed her. The woman picked out a shirt and undergarments. "Oh yeah, and I need a choker if you have one." The lady nodded her head and picked out a black ribbon choker that had nothing on it. When he paid, she smiled. He walked out of the door and went back to the blacksmith. "I just got your cross done Sir, however, you have to tell me if this is the size that you wanted. He brought out a 1 ½ sized cross; when the man looked at it a smile came to his face. The boy knew he did a good job. He brought out the silver bullets and that made the man even happier.

"Willson, you did well for yourself, now there is one more thing I need from you. I need you to make a pure silver moon. It has to fit on these black ribbons, and I will pay you twice the amount for your work. The man told him and of course, the boy's face lit up with joy. "What kind of moon do you want sir?" he asked. The man told him to do what he wanted to do. "I need that by the end of the day as well" he called over his shoulder. It was two hours before he went back to the suite. He knocked on the door and called out, "you dressed?" the girl did not answer. He knocked again this time the door cracked open. There were no sounds coming from inside the room, no lights were on. The man pulled out his gun and slowly walked in. He looked around the room where there were scratch marks on the wall, and the lamp was busted and water was all over the floor. There was no sign of the girl anywhere. He looked on the ground and saw water tracks everywhere. He walked around to the bed he spotted the girl, she was not dressed and was crying.

"What the hell happened here?" he asked and all the girl could do was point at him. However, he knew that it was not him she was pointing at so he turned around and saw nothing. He felt something drip on him; he looked up and saw a blanket of skin on the wall. "Shit, who was that?" he turned around and grabbed the blanket of the bed. He wrapped the girl and carried her out the door. He went into the bar. "What does your town not have traps or any security? Some beast attacked my daughter. What are you going to do about that?" the man yelled out. The bartender glanced at the bundle that was in the man's hands. "Is she all right?" the bartender asked. "Yeah barely, by the way, who is in charge of your town's headcount?" the man told him in an angry voice. "No one why?" the bartender asked, as he came to the man with the blanket.

"Take your daughter and go to the back. There you will find a room with a bed. I will call the doctor" he told him. The man nodded his head and walked behind. "Oh before I forget, or the intruder gave us a present, you might want the sheriff to take it out. It might give you a hint of the murder of that girl," he told the bartender. "Of course, but may I get your name sir." the bartender asked. The man turned his head. "If you need a name, call me Fang, but my real name has no meaning to you villagers," the man said. He went in the back and found the room, and he sat the girl on the bed. He unwrapped her face, and took his hands, and cuffed them around her face. "This is what I need you to do. I need you to get dressed in these." he put the new clothing on her lap and then coffed his hands back over her face. "After you are done knock on the door so I know I may come in. After you do so I will take you to get something to eat. Then I will allow the doctor to look at you. Then I want you to get some sleep. I will be here with you, so don't worry about getting hurt. Do you understand?" all the girl did was nod.

He started to head out the door when he heard her say. "Why did you call me your daughter?" the man looked around. "Because I am going to take care of you from this day on. That is why I called you my daughter, though if you don't want me to I can call you something else." he told her and then he went out the door. Adieu did not hear him walk away, which made her feel safe. She unwrapped herself from the blanket and got dressed in her new cloth. She did not mind being called another's daughter. Once she was done getting dressed she went over to the door and knocked twice. The door opened and Fang walked in. "Wow, you look nice, now for one more thing. Fang reached into his pocket and pulled out the black ribbon.

He walked towards Adieu, for a while she was scared of what he was going to do but all he did was tie the black ribbon around her neck. Once he was done he took her by the hand, and they both walked out and into the bar. The girl looked around, she saw men drinking, smoking, and laughing and smiling at her. All she did was smile back, then walked out the bar door. In her head, she was thinking to herself.*what's going on? No one ever smiled at me, nor let me inside a building. Something strange is going on.* Fang joined her a few minutes later. "Something wrong?" he asked. All she could do was shake her head no. Even though she wanted to say yes. Fang sighed, and then he started walking off. The girl followed right behind him. "So what do people call you around here?" he asked her.

"Nothing, they won't talk to me, let alone let me inside. That was the first time I was in a home, in any building," she told him. "Do they know your name?" he asked. "I don't know, I don't think so. When they found me they asked who I was. But before I had the chance to say anything. Someone said I had the mark, then everyone left me. Ever since then no one will talk to me. The only people that do are you and the village storyteller." she answered. For a while, he didn't say anything and all she did was look at him. "Do you have a name?" he asked.

"Yeah, everyone has a name. Mine is Adieu though I don't know my last name," she answered. "Your name is farewell?" he asked. "And what of it?" she asked, a little annoyed at Fang's remark. "Nothing, I just wondered why your parents called you that," he told her. They did not speak for a while, all they did was grab a hot dinner of beef and potato soup and rolls. After they were done eating they went to the doctors, where Adieu was checked. "Can you tell me what happened?" the doctor. "Yeah, how much do you want to know," she asked. "How about, what you were doing when you were attacked." the doctor suggested. Both Fang and the girl sighed; this is going to take a while to get used to. *I have no idea what to say to him.* she thought to herself and then looked at the one called Fang, when he just nodded his head she started telling the doctor everything that went on.

CHAPTER FOUR
In Hot or Cold Water?

"I was just getting my bath when I felt like someone or in this case something was watching me. So I looked around the room but did not see anything. So I got out and dried off. The next thing I knew a growl came from behind me, I looked right around and saw a creature that looked like a man and half wolf. It had sharp teeth like glass and eyes were like poodles of blood. The first thing I wanted to do was panic but something told me not to. All I remember doing is running around the room trying to stay away from it. Then when I hid behind the bed, I thought I was done for it, however, it pulled itself self-back and latched itself on the ceiling, and shed its skin. But when it did that there nothing was left." Adieu told the doctor.

My dear child, did you hit your head." the doctor asked her. "My daughter had a long day, however, she is no liar, what she said about the shedding is it's still in the room I think." Fang interrupted. The doctor left it at that and said that there were no injuries, so she may go. As they left Adieu pulled Fang aside. "Sir, do you think this will happen again?" she asked. Fang sighed and told her nothing and walked away. Not knowing what she should, she just walked behind him. The next thing she knew was they were back at the suite. The girl stopped in her tracks, she would not go back into that place even if those grey demons came back. Fang took notice of this, "you may stay out here, I will only be back in a few minutes," he told her.

He walked in and saw the maid cleaning the place up. "The room will be done in an hour, then you can rest up," she told him. Fang grabbed a case and turned to the maid. "My daughter and I will not be staying here, nor in this town, I will not have my daughter attacked again. All because a town has no defense for beasts roaming their town. I am disappointed in this lazy town anyway. Good day!"Fang exclaimed to her. The maid was speechless at the man's outrage, Fang walked out the door and motioned Adieu to follow him.

They walked to the blacksmiths and picked up the silver moon charm. Fang tied the moon charm on the girl's black ribbon then paid the boy. "Thank you for your hard work. Would you know where I can get a wagon to the next town?" he asked the young blacksmith. The young boy pointed to the wagon station Fang started walking away and then turned back to the boy, "Do you have any paper and ink on you?" He asked the boy. The young boy nodded his head and pulled out plane paper and a quill for the man. Fang took a few moments and wrote something down onto pieces of paper on both sides and then folded them in thirds and handed everything to the boy. "I need you to do me one more thing, I need you to take this to the mayor. It's informing him about the demons and who to contact about them so what happened in this town will never happen again," Fang told him. The boy smiled again and when Fang went to pay the boy again he held up his hand and put a close sign on his stand and ran off.

With this Fang took the girl and walked to the station and after a few moments, both of them were on their way. The girl was so happy to finally get out of that town and yet felt a bit sad to leave her home, that she looked out the window space and watched the buildings pass her by. To her, it was like the wooden cage door flung open, and with the wind celebrating her freedom. Though from her exaction of the long day of running for her life, the dinner, and doctor. Adieu fell asleep as soon when she was out of the town. Fang took off his buffalo skinned coat and draped it over her. She dreamed about the shadowed man, and the demons, also about her attack, but ended with a strange white light, with a gold cross in the middle of it.

CHAPTER FIVE
Dessert of Trust

On the wagon, Fang kept a close eye on the girl he found in Babylon village. *Adopting a child was not in my plans. But I couldn't let her stay there in that condition. It would not have been right to leave her there, though this is going to be a lot of work, I know nothing about girls. Why would she be attacked but not eaten like the rest of its victims?* he thought to himself. He looked at the sleeping girl next to him. "Your daughter is quite the lady." Fang heard one of the passengers say. He looked up to see a mother with her five-year-old son. "You think so; I thought she would need some work," He responded. The woman laughed, "How old is she?" she asked. Fang's expiration changed and he looked right back at Adieu. "I have no idea her age. I just picked her up today," he whispered two himself. Lost in thought with every detail on the girl that he heard from the woman, and the girl herself. However, nothing came to his mind with her age. *Maybe I should ask her one of these days.* he thought to himself.

He looked at the woman, "I have no clue, I just adopted her three hours ago, this village is anything but Babylon if they allow a young girl to sleep in the dirt." he told her. All the woman did was nod her head and smile. She looked at her son "I just got him three days ago, although I wanted a girl though I fell in love with this young boy." she told him. All Fang could do was smile at the woman, he looked back at the girl that had her head on his shoulder. *why did the beast not eat her, like it would do the rest? What caused it to back away from her?* Finally, in his train of thought, he closed his eyes and did not open them again. In the short time of his sleep. A world of pure light fields his mind. "Where am I, and what am

I going on," he asked himself. "You're out of time, you need to go back." a voice comes from the background. He looked around but could not see anything or anyone around him.

An unfamiliar blood-curdling scream came into play, He opened his eyes to find the woman clinging to the five-year-old boy. He looked to the left side of him. And found the girl was no longer there. "What the hell," Fang blurted out. "What happened where she is?" he asked the woman. The woman just pointed at the window. Fang looked and saw the wagon was surrounded by demons. "I thought they only came out at night," he said to himself.

The next thing anyone knew was a scream from the driver, and the horses crying out in fear. With the massive force of the jolt tipped over the wagon. All three were flung to the left side. Fang shielded the women and the boy from the blow of the window pane. With the woman and child fall on top of him, the pain went through his back; the air was snatched from his lungs. He could barely move with the lack of air and the weight that was upon him. He opened his eyes to see the demons lurking their way into the wagon. The woman screaming the little boy crying the sound drawls the demons towards the fallen fighter of the night. For the fallen fighter's cross was hidden in the right side pocket, it shall not show. All he could do was pray in his head. "God, I do not care if I live, but please help these people. Please help the girl and this family to live. I ask for nothing in return. The only thing that I ask is to help the girl on her way." His eyes closed and nothing more was said for the demons were all almost halfway in the wagon.

Adieu also had her problems; she was ripped out of the wagon. She woke up in the desert sand dunes. She started to get up when she heard snarling and growling around her. She looked up and found herself surrounded by demons. However they would not attack her, nevertheless they were very edge about something. To keep herself calm Adieu clenched her right hand. But instead of sand, it was something hard. She raised her hand to see what it was still keeping eye contact with the beast. The only thing she had in her hand was Fangs gold cross that was around his neck. She quickly got to her feet still clinging to the gold cross. She started looking for the wagon, to her left about twenty feet away the wagon laid. Not really knowing really what she was doing, she pushed the demons in front of her away. For she had seen more demons climbing into the wagon. She ran as fast as she could to it. Getting close to the wagon she could hear the little boy screaming in panic, and his mother screaming for help, and what sounded like she was in pain. She closed her eyes for a moment, to pray, "God I don't care if you help me, but I need the strengths to help them." she called out to the Lord. She reached the wagon and grabbed the demon's feet and started pulling them out of the wagon and throwing them at the others that were almost behind her.

After throwing the other two out of the wagon and to the others. She realized that there was one more that she could not reach down from where she stood. So she ran to the other side of the wagon, put the cross in her mouth, and started climbing to the top. Once she was at the top, she walked swiftly and carefully to the window frame. She went down to her hands and knees, then went arms and chest into the wagon. She grabbed the demon by the feet, and the demon screamed in pain, crawling its way back around to the top. By the sight of this, she dropped the cross right on the demons back. At this, the demon screamed in worse pain and fell to the bottom of the wagon. Which of course made the woman and her son scream worse.

The sound of the demon's screams even made Adieu cover her ears and scream in pain. "God makes it stop," she yelled out. The next thing she knew was the screaming had stopped, from both ends. With her ears ringing she looked down and there on the boy's clothing, was dust where the demon had laid. Adieu looked behind her and the other demons were gone as well. She got up and looked around; they were nowhere to be seen. She turned right around to see the boy's head sticking out of the window. "Can you help us out of here?" he asked her. She really could not see so well; however, she put her hand in the wagon window so the boy could grab on. Even though his hand was shaking he grabbed on top of hers. She carefully pulled him out.

Then she looked down into the wagon and reached her hand for the woman, however, the woman did not grab it instead it looked like she was frightened to death. Adieu told the boy to keep a hold of her ankles and to pull her up when she gave him the signal.

With the boy's help, she was able to get his mother up, afterwards she looked down at Fang, she did not know if he was alive or dead. She climbed inside the wagon to help the man that gave her a chance. She put her hand two inches over his mouth, to make sure he was breathing. Then she tore the sleeves off her shirt and used them to cover the wounds on Fang's arms and leg. She lifted him up and called to the boy for help. He popped his head in to see what he could do, then he held out his hands and lifted fang up. Adieu carefully got on the side of the seats, and lifted Fang more, then finally climbed out and pulled him out. They dropped him to the dusty ground then the boy jumped off the wagon and the powdered sand danced into the air.

Exhausted from running away from demons and saving the other three that Adieu lost her balance and fell off the wagon herself. She laid there in a daze she covered in thick sweat from the death rays of the sun. Her mouth was dry like the desert sand underneath her body, and she felt like they were out of breath and out of time. *What is going to happen? I can't move yet I am the only one that can do anything. No one can carry me and Fang. I have to get up, I just have to get up*Adieu thought to herself as she forced herself up with every drop of energy she had left. Feeling dizzy she forced herself to stay up. She looked at the woman who was embracing her son in her arms and crying. Then she looked around for the one who called her daughter and he was still laying where they had dropped him.

"If I can get him either back to town or to the next town I think he could be saved," she told herself. She looked all around but could not indicate where she was. She looked at the wagon, she turned to the woman. "The town is that way. We need to keep walking, if we do not the demons will come back, and it will be worse at night. I need you to trust me on this." she told the woman. All the woman could do was hold on to her son and nod her head. Adieu looked back down to her wounded companion and lifted him over her shoulder as much as she could. She started walking straight, even though she had no clue what she was doing.

The day was long and wary, but she managed to keep herself, the woman, and the boy go. Her body was starting to give way with the heaviness of Fang on her back and the exhaustion from the heat. She was already tired from fighting the demons, and she looked at the cross that had burned the demon to its death. *This Gold metal sure came in handy, I wonder what it is?* she thought to herself. She looked at the woman's face scratched up and full of terror. She looked at the boy, however, he did not look scared, or even seem to be affected by what just happened to them. She noticed that his eyes were lit up with joy and not tears. "Look mom!" the boy shouted. "It's water!" he pointed out. Adieu looked straight to where the boy was pointing, and sure enough, she saw it too. It was a piece of green land with what looked to be water. "I am not the only one that sees green am I?" she asked the kid's mom. "I am glad I am not going crazy out here in this heat. I was going to say something but I did not want to, just in case it was a mirage." the woman cried out. "Will if we head towards it we can get some water, and rest in the shade for a while." said the five-year-old boy. The four of them walked towards the oases. Adieu did not care about resting however she knew that she could clean Fang's wounds and at least try to wake him up. After an hour of walking the four finally got to the oasis, the boy ran into the water when Adieu and his mother laid Fang in the shade under a tree. "I just hope those things don't come back," the woman said.

"Those things are called demons, at least that's what Fang calls them. I think we are safe for the time being, I don't feel any danger, though the best thing is not to be afraid it attracts them." Adieu told her while looking around, "However I don't think your son should be walking too far into the water, we're not sure how deep it goes."Adieu answered her. The mother got up and ran to the boy's side, while Adieu went to fetch water to tend to Fang's energies, "His wounds are deep I can't believe this, I don't have that much medical skill except what I have used on myself. I hope I can help him," She said to herself.

CHAPTER SIX
Is Prayer the Cure?

Adieu ripped her black shirt around her waist and used it as a rag. She washed the wounds upon the man's head, and then his chest. "How is he doing? The woman asked. "The wound on his head is not bad, but his chest.... If only I had a needle and string." she told the woman. "I have a sewing kit right here," she pulls out a small wooden box from the pocket of her skirt. "Will this help you?" the woman asked her in a worried voice. Adieu looked at it real quick and it was not a medical string however she nodded her head and took the box from the woman. It took a while to get his wound sewed up however with the light fading away as the sun went down it was getting much harder for her to see the wounds. The lady and her five-year-old son started to make a fire to dry off and to help shine more light. After Adieu finished up she handed the wooden box back to the woman with a smile. "Sorry ma'am I used up most of your string, but I want to thank you. I will try to replace the ones that I used up," she told the lady. "Don't worry about it Dear, just get to sleep, you're going to need it," the woman told her.

The night was long and even though she was so tired Adieu could not get to sleep, all she could do was watch the darkness around them. It was really quite like it was before a storm and what concerned her was the air had the same energy as it did when the demons attacked her village. She kept an eye on the woman, the little boy, and the one that had become her father the same day. The thoughts of the bones of the mayor's daughter came into the play. "That demon that attaches me today was most likely the same one that killed her," she told herself. "But how did this man know what these creatures were, and why does this piece of metal affect them so much?" she asked herself while fiddling with the gold cross in her pocket. "I hope he doesn't get mad at me for ripping the shirt he got me. I wasn't even thinking when I did that," she whispered to herself.

She got distracted by a shadow moving close to her. "It's OK I am not going to hurt you or your friends. I just want to rest," The shadow figure told her. Not willing to trust the words of this being she scooted next to the sleeping man; with her hand clenching the golden cross that was still in her pocket. "Who are you?" she asked the shadow figure. "I am a shadow, one that has lost his way into the dark part of this world and fighting to find some light," It told her. "What are you talking about there is light in this world all around you," She exclaimed. "Not for me my dear only darkness, will I better go, your friend is about to wake and I can't let an exorcist see me," the dark being said as he vanished before her eyes. Adieu could not help but think the shadows' voice sounded familiar to her, though she had no idea where or why.

What was he talking about? Adieu thought to herself. The next thing she knew something touched her shoulder. "Shouldn't you be asleep?" a voice asked behind her. She turned around and saw that Fang was setting up. "What couldn't sleep?" he asked again. All she did was shake her head no at him and looked away from him. "Are you all right?" he asked her in a painful yet concerned voice. All she could do was nod her head yes and continue looking out through the darkness where the shadow figure left. She took a big breath and then started talking to him about what had happened to them and where they were. "I see then he heard me then," Fang said with a sigh of relief. "I am sorry sir, but who heard you?" she asked him. "My god heard me, I asked that he kept you three safe even if that meant I did not make it," Fang told her. "I see, I asked him myself to do the same thing, I guess he heard both of us. Sir why did the demon burn when it was touched by this." She asked him while handing him the golden cross.

Fang took the gold cross from his new daughters hand and then placed it on his chest. "Adieu do you not know what this is?" All she did was shake her head no she had seen it before, but no one had ever taken the time to tell her what it was or what it was for. "This is a cross, this piece of metal symbolizes many things. Demons cannot stand the holy light or anything that represents our Lord. Therefore when an object that has been in the holy light or represents holiness touches the demons of the night they are banished from the earth and put back into the hell which they came. The funny thing is this cross was never used for good, it was always used for darkness." Fang told her. "What do you mean?" she asked him. "You see kid this cross was my master's cross, and he called it the devil cross for it is meant to be used for darkness only, the silver crosses are meant for the light. However, nobody ever knows why not even me." He told her and noticed her starting to yawn. "Anyway you should get some sleep. I will stay up and keep a lookout for anything tonight," Fang finished. Adieu just nodded her head and laid down on the ground next to the man she knows nothing about.

She is very odd, why is she not dead? It doesn't make any sense she should have been killed being pulled out of the carriage like that. I didn't even hear a scared tone in her voice. Though then again I have been out for a while so she had a chance to calm down. Fang thought to himself. "It's going to be a long night," he whispered to himself. After a few moments, he went to pick the girl up and had a sharp pain go across his chest. "That's right, I shouldn't even be alive myself, you made a lot of miracles yesterday didn't you, my Lord," Fang whispered. He then carefully got up and walked to the fire and picked up a burning stick and saw the mom with her son on her chest fast asleep. After that, he walked around the oasis and picked up some sticks for the fire. "I am surprised that they all made it here, I wonder who took charge after I blacked out? Knowing the kids they would be freaked out so it had to be the mother. I will have to thank her when she wakes up tomorrow," He told himself.

He then carried the wood back to the campsite where he placed them into the fire and then stood guard for the rest of the night. The only movements were from the leaves on the trees from the slight wind, and then after a few hours, the boy woke up to go to the bathroom. Fang got up from his spot and walked with the child who seemed to be happy.

"You're not scared?" Fang couldn't help but ask the boy. "No, I have that girl around me, I don't need to be afraid," The boy told him. "You should have seen that girl take care of those monsters, it was so cool," the boy told him while going behind a tree.

"So what happened?" he asked the boy. "Will, after the wagon tipped the monsters, started coming in, and that girl came and pulled them out away from us, afterward she got all of us out of the wagon. Of course, I helped, and I can sure say you are one heavy man, Sir."The boy told him in a very cheerful voice. Fang couldn't help but laugh a bit, "Sorry for that," he told the boy. "Will any way mommy was scared to death that she grabbed me and started crying, the girl was on the ground I thought maybe she had died until she somehow picked herself up from the ground. I watched her look around and then told mom and me that if we headed the way we came or at least try to get to the next village we would be safe." The boy told him.

"She carried you all the way here and then stitched you all up with mommy's thread." The boy told him. "Though mommy didn't let me watch, she told me to go play in the water while she took care of it." The boy told him while he came walking to Fang's side. "Sounds like you have a very smart mother," he told the boy. Both of them started walking back to the campsite in silence, once there the boy went back to his mother, and Fang sat back down next to Adieu and then continued watching everything in the night. After a few moments he then carefully placed his daughter's head on his lap so she wasn't breathing in the sand.

The wind was howling like it was in pain, the fire crackled as it was laughing at all of them for one day they all will burn. The chill of death lingered through their bodies and souls. The ground was still and quiet like they were forgotten by time and the lives of others. The darkness is slowly coming to an end, as the sun rose from its grave. It has been hours since they were there.

Now it was time to break the peace and enter the day of turmoil. Fang shacks the sleeping girl and brings her back into the world of the living.

Slowly she could hear him complaining about the ripped shirt pieces that were on his arms and legs. "I am surprised there is anything left on this kid, and looking at it she forgot to get my bag from the wagon," Fang's voice razed. "Be thankful that you're still alive, that girl saved your life. There was no time to get any bags, we were in a rush to get the hell out of there if you have forgotten we just got attacked," the woman scolded him with a vinacing voice.

"I did not forget about that, I just had stuff in that bag that was to be delivered to my order." He told her. "Well, then I guess you should have kept it on your back. What order are you from anyway?" she asked. Fang shook the girl once more, "I am from my god's order, no other." he tells the woman. "I see and who is your god?" she asked but before Fang could answer Adieu woke, "About time I swear you sleep like you're dead," he scolded her. "Sorry, I didn't mean to sleep that long. How are you feeling?" Adieu asked him while climbing to her feet. "I am fine, though the next time you want to bandage someone doesn't use your shirt. I don't want to keep buying you shirts." Fang said while taking off his jacket and handing it to her. "Put this on, you're revealing too much skin. Do you know where you left my bag? He asked her. "Sorry sir but no, I was too busy trying to get everyone out alive to think of the bags. It might take all day just to find them in this heat. Also, I don't think anyone wants to go back with those things out there. Even if I can send them away, I can't do it by myself again, it's just too much for one person to do," she told him. "Well, this ground is somewhat holy so the mother and the child should be fine here by themselves. You and I need to go get those bags, I have some important things in mine," he told her.

"OK, if I had to guess I would say we just kept going straight from the carriage. However I can't tell you how long we walked for before we got here," Adieu told him. "That's fine it at least gives us a route to go by, however, we don't have any way to carry water with us. Are you going to be all right with that?" Fang asked her. "I should be fine. I am used to not having water in me for the longest time. However those things are still out there, I don't know how to fight them off very well." She told him. With that Fang took off the gold cross from his chain around his neck, "Take this and don't lose it, it seems to help you out more than it does me. HoweverI want it back after we are done with this?" he tells her. "Yeah, I got it." She answered him with a sigh as she put it in her pocket, after getting a few drinks of water both of them left the woman and the child by themselves. Though they could hear the mother's protest of Fang taking her with him.

The scorching sun beats down on the dusty sand. The wind passes by them as a silent whisper, and time becomes slower to the point of nonexistence. Several hours went by without any words being spoken and each footstep became a mile. No man nor beast was seen for miles which were all good for them. Finally, they came to the wagon, Adieu looked around and saw no one around. There was no corps of the driver or the two horses. The wagon itself would not be able to be fixed. "They made a mess out of the thing, didn't they?" Adieu called out to Fang. "Yes they did, they always do. However, they normally do worse than this. I wonder why we are all alive still," He told his new daughter. "And why was she not ripped to shreds? " he said to himself. Adieu walked towards him, "They're, not the only ones, are they? Because they did not look like the ones from two nights ago and in the hotel room," She asked them.

"No, there are more than the Bone Eaters." Fang started to explain. "What is the thing that attacked us called Bone Eaters?" she asked him. "Well you see the bone eaters are the easiest ones to attract, however, they are almost the hardest to kill. Though if you get them from behind with holy water or silver or in your case a gold cross and they will burn." He explained to her. "Is there anything that keeps them away?" She asks as she walks to the ravage. "There is always something however it never stays long enough and it only works in homes. Burn white sage keeps them away for a while however people stopped using it when it kept burning the senses. Another thing is water; however we are in a desert that has only one water source around, and that's the one that we just came from," He explained to her.

After a while of looking around, they are able to find all the bags. "So what attracts the Bone Eaters?" Adieu asked her adopted father. "Will the main attraction for them is the scent of fresh blood, To come to think of it I was stupid for bringing you out here with your wounds, however, if we stayed there in the village the town would have been covered with them in a matter of minutes," Fang told her while picking up his bag. He shuffled through his bag and pulled out a packet of papers. "Good they are still there. OK shall we get back to the others?" he asked her. "Yes sir, we should I just hope we don't run into them again." She told him. "There is no reason you should fear them, even if they crawled out of the flesh of man. For those who trust in the Lord will have him around to protect them all the way through," Fang told her. She stopped in her tracks while her new father walked ahead of her. "He won't with me," she mumbled out with a sharp pain through her own heart. It took a while before Fang noticed she was walking behind him anymore.

"You know if you are going to continue to do this all the way, we are going to run into them again." He yelled out to her. Then he noticed she was not paying any attention to his words; she was in her own little world. "For heaven's sake will you get a move on?"Fang yelled higher to her. Adieu heard him but still could not bring herself to move from the spot that was pulling her down back into the darkness letting her know that she would never leave the side of the Devil himself for he had marked her as his. Fang became angry with his adopted daughter and went back and grabbed her hand and dragged her ruthlessly across the desert sand. He only stopped when she pulled her hand away from his. "What can't handle the fact someone touching you?" he hissed out without meaning to. "I was told that God won't lay his genital hand on me for I am the Devil's child," she said as she took her hands behind her neck and untied the black ribbon with the silver moon.

"For he has marked me with his fangs," she continued as she threw her hair away from her neck and showed the curse mark. Fang looked right at his new daughter's neck and then looked away from her not sure what he was going to say to her. "Please put your ribbon back on," He told her. She did as she was told, and put her collar back on, then started walking ahead of her step-father. Fang then followed his adopted daughter and he couldn't figure out what to tell his new daughter. "Who told you that God won't lay his hand on you?"Fang finally asked. "The village Priest that use to take care of me before something attacked him." She told him. "You believe that he wouldn't?" Fang asked her. "Why would he, I am an abomination to him and his children, I was born of the devil flesh," Adieu told her step-father. "And yet you pray to him," Fang pointed out to her.

"Because I pray for other people not for myself," she told him. "You make no sense to me kid," he told her and continued walking behind her. After a few hours went by Adieu started lagging behind her step-father again, but instead of getting mad at her he just walked slowly. After a while Fang stopped and waited for her to get right next to him, he then picked her up and put her on his back. Even though his wounds stung with pain from the extra weight he didn't put her down. After walking in silence for a while Fang started talking to her again, "You know I have read about the Devil's mark for his children and three holes behind the neck is not one of them," he told her. He waited for her to say something but she never did so he continued talking to her, "His mark is three numbers and they are 666, and if you don't, believe me, it's within the bible," He told her.

Even though he told her this truth he knew she would not believe him right away, he looked part way up to see the look of doubt in her eyes and smiled then looked away and kept walking. "Another reason to believe me is if that was a mark of the devil then I would have killed you by now and would not be taking care of you like this."He told her. After a while, he stopped talking and just continued to walk the way they came and finally came to the oasis where the boy and his mother stood waiting for them. "For goodness sake, I thought you passed out from your wounds," she yelled at him and then noticed the girl on his back. "Is she all right?" she asked him while helping her off of Fangs back. "Yeah she just got tired so I carried her. You both look refreshed at least," Fang told her. "Yes, well there was nothing to do but rest here," she said. Not even five seconds of getting Adieu on the ground the boy latched his arms around her, "Mama wouldn't let me go after you," he told her. "Your mama is a smart lady after all those things are still out there," Adieu told him. Fang handed the woman her cloth bag and a brown suitcase, "I believe these are yours, "Fang told the woman, and with a smile, the woman accepted the bags.

Adieu couldn't figure out when he grabbed the lady's bags but figured that maybe it was when she was not paying attention. "So what are we going to do now? We can't stay here, there is not enough food here, and the food we have here is no bigger than our pinkie," the woman told him. "OK I just need to rest a few minutes and while I rest I will try to come up with a plan," he told the woman. With that Adieu watched as her new father sat under a tree and then laid against and closed his eyes. Then Adieu stood there for a few seconds before the woman walked up to her and started complaining, "Thinking! He isn't thinking of a way out of this dessert he is taking a nap, why are men, such liars? Tom will you get out of the water!" she yelled out. With that Adieu decided to sit next to her step-father and wait until he was well-rested. "That woman is an annoying one isn't she," Fang asked her. Adieu wanted to laugh but figured that it wouldn't be a good idea and just smiled. "How are you feeling?" Fang asked her. "Shouldn't I be asking you that, you're the one with most of the wounds," she pointed out to him. "I am fine, I have had worse within my line of work, I just need some time to rest and that woman's yelling is not helping." He told her.

"She is just worried, it is normal for a woman to worry, especially if she has a child with her. A woman's mind can go right into a panic, overprotective, or bossy," Adieu told her new father. Fang just looked at his daughter a little surprised, "Do you really know that, or is that what you hope for?" he asked her. "I know for a fact from watching the townspeople," she told him while turning around and not facing him. I always envied the other kids for they had someone that would take care of them, almost every woman in town was a mother to everyone except for me. Though without knowing it completely they raised me or maybe they did know and just wouldn't anyone else know," Adieu told him. "I guess any kid that lived the way you have would wish for that to be true," Fang told her. Adieu then turned and faced the water, but it didn't take long for her to notice that something red started flickering in it. "Fang what is that out in the water?" she asked while pointing to it. "Most likely a school of redfish," Fang told her and closed his eyes once again. Though for some reason she could not believe that and kept looking at it, and then noticed that the red flickers were rising out of the water.

"Fang I don't think those are fish," she told him while getting up. Fangthen looked at the flickers of red and noticed she was right. He quickly got up and grabbed his daughter by the arm and started walking towards the dessert. "I need you to start walking into the desert and do not look back for any reason, if we get separated I will find you. If you get to a wall of iron, find the gate and let them know that you are to meet Father Fang by the holey fountain, do you understand?" he told her. "Yes Sir," she answered and started walking, never looking back to see what was going on with the others, though she knew that Fang wasn't going to leave them. After a while she heard the boy and woman crying and hollering, she had no idea what was going on and if Fang was all right, all she knew was she had to take the man's instructions. She walked swiftly through the desert and did not stop for a second, the sky became an amber red and quickly turned into the crimson sun, which in her village meant that someone died that day in a brutal fashion. She could only pray that it was none of the three that was traveling with her. The only time that she stopped was when the feeling of danger left her heart and by past experience, she knew that meant that she was completely safe to take her time, though she still did not look back.

CHAPTER SEVEN
Demon's Called Men

After a little time of resting Adieu started walking once more not sure which way she was going. All she knew was she had to find the Iron Gate and meet Fang at the fountain if she could make it. She felt like every second she had been walking was like an hour within the day and after two hours of walking straight was like a mile. She was running low on energy from lack of food and water, and the sun beating on her didn't help matters. By the time the sun sat she collapsed into the sand where she lay nearly frozen to the ground and had no idea if she was going to make it through the night. At this moment in time, Adieu didn't even care if a demon came her way for she couldn't help but think maybe death would be more lenient than living. Though for some reason she scolded herself for even thinking that and found a bit more strength to get up and continue walking. She started staggering across the dark desert not really caring which way she was going but her foot at the edge of a sand dune which made her fall to her left and roll all the way down to the sanded valley and just laid there. The last thing she saw was a light and a dark figure walking towards her before she gave way into the darkness of her soul.

When she woke back up she found that her hands and legs were bound and her eyes were blindfolded. Having no idea what was going on she felt her heart beating faster, and she was about to start struggling until she remembered what the dark figure in her box tent told her. *If I am not careful those demons will return. All I have to do is stay still and learn what's going on around me and try not to make any sound.* she thought to herself. So she laid there lessening she could hear creaking and she recognized it from the wheels of the wagon that she was in with Fang. She could smell a thick layer of iron in the air and she knew right then that someone or something was either dead or hurt badly. *This not good that could track those blood demons,* Adieu thought to herself but still kept herself calm. "Hi, Nail I think we may have picked up a dead one she ain't moving," She heard a man's voice.

"No, she is alive, though I doubt that one boy is going to live much longer. We should just throw him off the carriage," She heard another man call from the horse's seat. "Will if he lives he won't catch much of a price like this sweet one," She heard the man's voice and then felt something stroke her face. "Mill don't touch the merchandise!" She heard another man with a hoarse voice. "Yes sir," that she heard was footsteps moving away from her but she could feel eyes piercing through her like hot pokers. Adieu was so used to the feeling but this time it was like death was upon her with his seethe at her throat.

She gave death a slight smile and told him she was ready whenever he was just not to let it hurt. Though death did not answer her or even acknowledge her, though as fast as he came he vanished without a signal trace. Adieu waited until she felt no one watching or their presents before she struggled out of the ropes that bound her and then quickly took off the blindfold. there was slight blinding of light and then she was able to see. She looked around and she was in a wagon with a few boxes behind her. on both sides there were chains, whips, swords, and a few other things that Adieu had no idea what were. When she followed her nose to where the iron was she found a young man tied with a gash in his side.

The only thing she could think of was she needed to get the bleeding to stop before he attracted any demons. She looked around some more and found some string and a curved small hook. She quickly used them to sew up this man's wounds and then used a cream-like cloth and bound it uptight."I hope you wake up soon so I can ask you some questions. "She whispered to the young man. "I am awake and you were stupid for moving around like this," The man whispered back to her. "Excuse me for trying to save you, plus trying to keep the demons at bay." She told him. He really didn't say anything back to her, though she did not blame him. She kept a very sharp ear out for any strangers.

"Who has us?" she asked the young man. "They go by the name Kekewey. I really don't know the meaning of their name," He told her. "I know of them. My own village sold people that have done great wrongs to them because I was too young; they didn't sell me," she told him. "Then what are you doing here?" he asked her.``I fled from demons and got split up from father Fang," she told him while hoping that her new father was safe. "What's your name kid?" the young man asked her. "Adieu," She answered him and she could tell he was fighting the urge to laugh"Will excuse me for having an odd name," She hissed at him."Sorry I should not make fun of the one who tried to help me."He told her while trying to get up before she placed her hands on her chest. "You really should not try to move, you might have lost a lot of blood." She told him. "I have not lost that much blood yet," he told her while standing up and slowly moving her behind him. Adieu was slightly confused but didn't bother asking why because she could hear someone come back in.

CHAPTER EIGHT
Slavery Wagon

"Where is the girl!?" she heard the man ask with a very angry voice. "I told you to tie her up!" She heard a voice she didn't hear the last time. "I did," She heard the one called Nail, "Its not my fault that Mill decides to use a knife to cut her clothing!" he told the other voice. "Mill is the psycho person but he knows not to mess with the merchandise. "I don't know what to tell you she was right there," the man said in a very annoyed voice. "Where is the Boy?" Nail asked subordinate. "Now I know for a fact he is not able to go far," the second man told his boss. With that Adieu heard rushing footsteps around the wagon. "I can not believe this first the girl goes missing and now the boy who do you think is going to get in trouble for this hmm? Who do you think is going to have their head on the chopping block if we don't have the goods? It will be mine and guess who will be coming with me to hell?" Nail yelled at his subordinate.

"Sir there is no way they are not on this wagon we would have seen them get off. They must be behind the boxes," the second man told him. "Will you better be right or you will die right here and now!" the one called Nail yelled out of anger and with that Adieu heard the doorsteps disappear and all she could do was look at the man standing in front of you her. "We need to get off this wagon quickly," the man told her. "I know I need to get back to Hang or at least get to the iron gate," she told him. "The Iron Father's I Know where that is, but I thought women were not to be there?" the man told her. "Really don't know, Fang just told me to meet him there," she told him. "Will if we get out of here I will help you get there for payment for fixing my leg," he told her as he looked around the creates. "We will have to wait for darkness before going anywhere," the man told her. "That is going to be hell, demons come out at night," she told him and he smiled and sat down and started waiting.

Adieu could hear the men yelling and screaming because they could not find her. "Who are they," she asked them. "They are slave traders, they capture or buy people and sell them into slavery," the man told her. "That's horrible, why would anyone do that?" She asked. "One-word greed, they love money so much they do not care how they get it." the man told her and all she could do was stare at him. "How old are you?" the boy asked her though she did not speak she only shook her head. She really did not know how old she was. "I see what can you tell me about yourself?" the man asked. "Not much I have been on my own since I was five, and the villagers have been afraid of me. I was adopted by Father Fang I think a week ago," she told him and all he did was smile. "What is your new father like?" he asked her. Adieu thought for a moment before she answered. "He gets mad easily though he is very kind. He risks his own life before allowing anyone to get hurt. The last time I was with him he was hurt really bad." she told him and then became silent hoping that he was OK. "I will get you to that metal gate even if it kills me. No one should be away from their family and be sold for any reason," the boy told her.

Adieu, and the boy waited till no one was moving around or far away yelling to come up with an escape plan. "You're injured so you may bring demons here tonight," she told him. "That is what I counting on," the boy told her with a slight grin. She was not too sure what to make of him and was not sure if this was a good idea. The only thing she knew was they could get away with all the confusion. "What if someone is guarding the door?" She asked him. "That's why I want you to wait in here until I give you the signal to come out." He told her. "Ok I guess I understand," she told him before he quickly covered her mouth with his hand. "She is nowhere to be found," one of the men shouted. "She is a small malnourished child. She is probably dead out there already," someone yelled out to them.

"You're most likely right, Thankfully we still have the boy," one of the people laughed out. "Yeah well, I doubt he would fetch a good price.

I would be surprised if he gets bought for a hundred." another man told the other. The boy uncovered her mouth slightly when she gripped his arm slightly and pulled down on it. "You will be alright," the boy told her. Adieu couldn't help but believe this boy, though she was also determined to live and get to the iron gate and make sure that Fang was OK. Before she had a chance to go over the plan in her head the boy grabbed her and jumped out of the wagon. They both rolled for a while as he kept her tucked under his chest.

After they stopped he whispered in her ear, "Let's go." before taking her hand and dragging her behind him. It did not take long for the slave traders to go after them. Adieu Looked down and the moonlight showed the blood seeping through the boy's bandages and then they heard a loud screech and then the men behind them screaming. "Dame those things are fast," the boy shouted. "Just don't stop running," Adieu told him while trying to keep calm.

"Girl you should worry about your own skin at this point," the boy told her. She was going to say something back but he started speaking once more, "I am able to fight these demons."

Adieu had no chance to ask him what he meant by that before he yanked her arm and she landed right in front of him. When she looked she saw a spark of light went around them, "They can't pass heaven's wall!" he shouted to her. "heavens will" she whispered to herself. The boy bent down and pulled her into his chest, "It's a gift I was born with, my village told me, God, himself smiled on me," He told her. "I think I would call it the wall of screaming," she told him while trying to cover her ears. She managed to look over his shoulder and through the light and sand. What she saw was the Demons burning in flames.

She couldn't help but feel a bit alarmed by this boy's power. It did not take long before all the demons turned to ash. The light faded and then the wall was gone. "Are you OK?" he asked while letting go of her. "I think so, though I can say I have never seen that before," she told him while sitting on the ground. "Sorry I hope I didn't scare you," while Collapsing to the ground.

"Are you OK?" Adieu asked him while taking his hand. "Yeah it just wears me out very much, I will be OK for a few minutes," he told her.

"Who are you?" she asked him while she rebandaged the wound. "My name is Sai," he told her while watching her and keeping an out into the night. "Well Sai, I am glad they were not able to sell you," she told him while tightening the bandage. The boy just laughed while she stared at him with a confused look. "Sorry I didn't mean to laugh, however, my village did sell me. I can't blame them, they needed the money!" he told her. "You are OK with that?" she asked him in an odd voice. "To tell you the truth no, but I understood their reasoning. I guess you might say I have forgiven them." Sai told her." I don't know how you did that, but I guess that means you have a good heart." she told him. "I don't know about a good heart or not, I just know this world is filled with hate and our lives are too short to hold grudges," he told her.

"I guess you are right though we need to start getting out of here before the demons come back," she told him. "I agree but with my leg, I am not sure if we would make it," he told her. "That's OK I will carry you there, besides your side wound looks like it's doing better," Adieu told him with a smile though she had no idea if he could see it within the dark. "Very well I did promise I would get you to the Iron gates. Though I do not know if they will let you in for you are a woman." Sai told her. "That's OK, he just told me to get there and tell them Father Fang sent me," She told him.

CHAPTER NINE
The Journey Through the Desert

Adieu helped him up with the only concern of getting him out of the darkness with his fresh injury. She was not sure if she would be able to protect him as he did her and she did not know where she would be heading. "Any ideas on where we are to go?" she asked him with a nervous laugh. "No I just know its to the north of my village," he told her while slowly taking steps. "Great will lets hope we heading the right way," Adieu told him while taking small strides for him to be able to keep up with her. Every howl in the darkness her strides became a little faster each time she took a step. They only stopped short enough for both of them to catch their breaths and figure out which way they would try next. "Sia, when your village found out you were different, were they scared of you?" she asked him trying to come up with a faster way to kill time.

"Some did but after a while, they warmed up. My village took care of everyone around them even if they were passing by." Sia told her as he limped with her. "Sounds nice I wish I could see your town," she told him. "How about you and your town," Sia asked her. "My town is somewhat peaceful but they don't take care of outsiders very well," she told him while placing him on the ground. "Sorry I need a rest," she pointed out while sitting on the ground. "It's all right don't over do it," he told her while seeing her pale face from the moonlight. "Are you going to be alright?" he asked her. "Yeah I'm fine just need to rest that's all," she told him through the truth was she was feeling weak from hunger though she knew she should be used to it. Before she knew it Sai grabbed a hold of her and pulled her onto his lap. "Then rest for a few and I will keep guard," he told her, and before she could say anything to him her eyes closed and her soul went into the darkness.

When she woke she noticed that he was carrying her on his back. "What are you doing? You are hurt you should not be carrying me like this," she told him. Sia laughed, "You should be more worried about your own self there hun. you were running a fever there is no way I could allow you to carry me like that." he told her while continuing to walk. "It's almost morning you should get some more sleep while you can," he told her. With that, she closed her eyes once more but then she felt a different present around them. "Sia I don't think we are alone," she whispered to him. "Ah you felt it as well then, you're a smart girl just keep quiet and act like you're sleeping we will be fine," he told her. "How do you know?" she asked him, "Because I have dealt with it once already tonight," he told her.

With that Adieu reclosed her eyes but could not shack the uneasiness that was coming closer to them. "Dame I don't think we are going to shake them this time," she heard Sia tell her. "Demons?" she asked. "Yeah and not the good kind, and I have not recuperated from the last time," Sia told her. "You need to put me down," she told him. "You're joking right, I am going to keep walking away from them not stopping to put you down," he told her. "Then loosen your grip," she warned. "I am not having you fall," he told her. "Please stop arguing with me, if they grab me you don't need to be pulled back to!" Adieu whispered in an angry voice. With that Sia slightly loosened his grip around her legs but she knew he was not happy about this.

With a single snarl, Adieu felt a sharp tug on her shoulder followed by pain when she hit the ground on her left side. When she looked she saw the demon turn to ash, though she had no idea what to do because she did not have Fang's cross on her anymore. She had no idea how to help Sha out either, 'If there is a God out there please keep the boy safe.' Adieu preyed. She was surrounded and when she looked at Sha he was surrounded as well. The state of panic was close to kicking in when she noticed a slight grin forming on his face. Before she knew it a stream of light flowed around him and slowly came to her.

When the light touched her she heard a scream within her head and pain hit her entire body. Without screaming in pain Aduie kneeled down in pain. Her neck burning where she had been bitten felt as if it was being ripped off before he hit the ground with her whole body. Though what she saw was the boy standing in front of her with what looked to be a pure white wing and him kneeling down to take a hold of her. as soon as his hands were wrapped around her the pain faded away. "Stay with me," she heard the boy order her before she passed out once more.

"Hold on kid I've got you," She told her while picking her up and holding her close to his chest. "I guess it's a good thing that she is unconscious so I can get my full-strength out without hurting her even more," he told himself. With that Sha released all his spirit energy and made the wall a lot bigger and with every demon that it hit they turned to ash. He walked within the direction of the Iron gate holding the worn-out child in his arms. He kept his wall up until they came to the Oasis where Audie last saw Fang. He placed her onto the ground and gathered water in his palm and carefully walked it over to her. He placed his hands to her mouth and let the water trickle down her throat.

"Come on please wake up, you still have things to do within this lifetime," he told her. With a grunt and her head moving to the left and gasped for air and then coughed. Her eyes opened for a few seconds and then closed once more and slumbered on Sai's lap. "Good her life is not in any danger, I will rest here for a moment and then get her to the Iron gate. I just hope they let her through after all no woman has ever passed those gates for thousands of years," he told himself, and with that Sai leaned against the tree and closed his eyes to rest. He slept for a few hours and then took the sleeping girl and placed her on his back and walked across several miles of sand under the scorching sun.

Even though he was drained by the heat had never stopped once and continued walking. After a few more steps he found a new town that was only three miles away from the Iron gates. There he found a new green shirt for her and some bandages to wrap both their wounds. He kindly worked on repairing a few things for the shopkeeper in exchange for the items he needed. He also grabbed them both some bread and milk for them to eat, and did chores around the inn so they had a place to stay. They stayed there while she rested and recovered her strength. Audie waited in the room while Sai did his jobs when he came back he always looked tired but he always looked tired. "Sha when can we get to the Iron gate?" she asked him. "Hopefully in a few days you look like you are almost well enough to get going again. Thankfully there have been no demons coming through this town." Sai told her. "That is always a good thing, but are you sure you are all right with what you are doing? You always look so drained." Adieu informed him and all he did was laugh. "If I don't work then we don't have a place to stay while you rest," he told her.

After a few days, Adieu was back on her feet and helping Sha earn money for the rest of their journey. Though secretly she was saving most of it to pay her new father back for the gold cross that she had lost. It was a nice feeling for people not to be scared of her, but she also felt odd for she felt as if she was lying to this town. "Adieu the innkeeper needs some help with the floors today. Do you think you can do that for me? I would do it but I promised the Storekeeper that I would do his floors tonight when the store is closed," Sha told her. "It's no big deal, I will be glad to help with the floors," Adieu told him, and with that Sai took off to the store. Adieu quickly went downstairs and looked around for the innkeeper. "Oh you look like you're doing much better now," a man announced behind her.

"Are you the innkeeper?" she asked him.``I am the husband of the innkeeper. My name is Swingal," he told her. "Well, Mr. Swingal Sai asked me to help with the floors today." she told him "Oh I see, well then let us go get a bucket and cloth," he told her. They both walked around the inn to the cabinet that held the buckets and clothes and then he took them and filled them up with water and placed them around the inn for her to use. Adieu took each cloth and washed the floors it took her most of the day, and it wore her out completely. When the floors dried it really did not look as if she cleaned at all, surprisingly it looked worse. "How the heck did that happen?" she couldn't help but ask herself.

"What's the wrong dear?" a woman's voice came around the corner. "Oh My that horrible," the voice shrieked. "I'm sorry I have watched many women in my village do their porches but I think I did something wrong. However, the water is all dirty so I don't know how." Adieu told her. "Little lady has you ever cleaned anything?" she asked her. "No, first time, I thought it would be easy," Adieu told the woman. "Well Little lady, My inn is a high establishment and dirt has no place." Mr. Swingle told her.

"Sorry, Mr. Swingle, I never did this before, I thought I did what I watched the ladies of my village did," Audie told him. "Well then let's teach you the right way," he told her and led her back to the cabinet that had the cleaning rags. The manager grabbed the empty buckets from the first time that she cleaned the floors and filled them once again. He then knelt on the ground with her and showed her how to clean the floors and after he knew she had a hang of it he left her alone. It took her longer this time however he was very pleased this time that he gave her 9 gold than what he told Sha which was 5 gold coins. She was also allowed to pick something from his small gift shop as a thank you which she tried to decline but he would not hear of it. So she looked at the jewelry and the hairpieces but did not like any of what she saw.

Sure they were beautiful and any normal girl would take them but she had no use for them. She looked at the pipes and the tobacco but she never liked the smell of them, then she came to the journals and quail's and she knew she did not know how to write or read but she figured that she could try her hand at it at some point. When she went to pick up a black leather journal she saw a small bag that she could use to carry food and other things that she and Sha would need. It was a green leather bag that had a silver leaf design on it. She handed it to the Innkeeper and he gave her a smile, "You should take this to keep your money in, make sure you keep it on your belt at all times that way no one can take it from you." Mr. Swingletold her and she gave him a smile. She then went up to their room and waited for the boy to come back from his job. She knew they would have to leave soon in hopes that Fang was at the Iron Gate and not mad at her for not being there. It was about three hours before Sai came back to the room where he then flopped onto the bed to catch a few zs. He only took thirty minutes to sleep and then packed his own bag and grabbed her and walked out the door with Aduie following him from behind.

They walked out of the sandy village and back into the desert where Aduie felt a huge dread come over her. Sai looked at her and then took her hand, there was no way he was going to let anyone or anything happen to her. They walked around the edge of the wall for the longest time. Adieu does your father know about your power?" Sai asked her. "I am not sure, I would be surprised if Fang didn't know about it. Heck, I don't even know if my village or real parents even knew that I had this in me. I never used it until Fang took me away from my village." she told him. Sai did not say anything after that, though she could tell he was in deep thought. It took about three hours before they cleared the walls of the village they just left.

They came to the wagon stop where they stood for a few moments to see if they could catch it to save time. Though Sai had enough of waiting and started walking once more. "How old are you?" Sai asked her while getting tired of the silence. "I am fifteen years of age," Adieu told him as she followed right behind him. "Well that is what my village told me," she pointed out to him.

"That young?" his voice sounded as if he was laughing. "I lost my parents when I was five years old. It has been ten years since then," she told him. "Wow sorry, then who razed you?" Sai asked her. "I lived in a box since I was five, though I guess that would be the whole village," she told him. "Sorry, I thought you would be twelve just by the way you look. I guess that means you really were not fed right," he told her. "Well I only got to eat what was thrown on the ground so yeah I guess," she told him, almost surprised that she never really thought about it. Sai tossed his head to the right to left as he thought more about what she was saying.

They only stopped once or twice to drink water from their canteens. "We should be there in three days by foot, thankfully there are towns where we can stop by," Sai told her. "That's if we don't get a wagon first?" Adieu couldn't help but ask in the middle of him explaining. "Yes," he told her "and if we go sparingly on our water we should make it to the village before we run out. We also have to be careful of the slave wagon," he pointed out. "Will how long do we have to get to the next village," Adieu asked him. " A few more hours, I think though I am not sure," Sha told her as he started walking again and they went quiet. They walked a few more miles when Aduie stopped before their time to stop again, She had a cold feeling as if she was being watched. "You all right?" Sai asked her. "Yeah I'm just tired I think," she told him, trying not to scare him.

"Are you sure?" he asked her, "Yeah," she told him. He started dragging her at this point though he kept her a bit closer to her, "Sha how long have you had your powers?" Adieu asked him. "Four years after my own parents died. I was razed by my village church, though that treated me like a blessing, not a cure," he told her. "My local pastor took care of me and helped train my powers," Sha told her. "My pastor tried to help me until my village called him the devil's helper," Adieu told him. After that, she stayed quiet while he did not say anything back to her though she could tell the way he held her hand he did not like what she had told him either.

CHAPTER TEN
Heated Rain

"Adieu, can I ask how you survived by yourself?" Sai asked her. "Well I had a hard time for a while but it got a bit easier after figuring out what and what not to do," she told him. "What do you mean," Sha asked her. "I learned what time to scavenge for food, clothing, and things to fix my boxed home. I used old notebooks to learn to write and tried to read. To be honest, I am not really good at any of it, but I know enough to make due. I watched my village women know how to act somewhat of a young lady though I saw no point in it. After all, I was nothing but a street rat to them, During the day I seemed human enough to them, though during the night it was like I was some sort of monster that was not to be trusted." she told him which I guess he did not like because he slightly squeezed my hand. "Well that is all in the past now and when I get back with Fang I will have a new life," she told him and he loosened his grip on my hand. "Sha can I ask what you will do after you are done getting me to the Iron Gate?" she asked him.

"I have no plan for my life, I was meant to be a slave to a master. However, that has been taken from me. After I am done with taking you, I must go find a caravan and see if they will take me to the slave town to see if I can regain my village honor." he told her. "Sha by all means the caravan has been destroyed to anyone you have died. Why not choose a new life for yourself and not worry about your town's honor? I mean they have the money already right?" She asked him. "You are right, but then I have no clue what to do," he told her with a slight side glance. They continued to walk in silence when Sai felt something hot fall on his cheek and stopped and looked up. Adieu was going to ask him what was up when it fell on her to when she touched her face it was liquid. "I thought it never rained in the desert!" she exclaimed and before she was able to say anything more Sha lifted her on his back and started moving faster. "Technically you are right, however when it does you don't want to be out in it," he told her in almost a shout.

Adieu kept an eye on her surroundings for a place for them to take shelter but it was the dessert not much was out there. She watched as the water hit the scolding sand that it turned into steam. "Sai what happens when it starts raining harder?" Adieu could not help but ask him. "You see the steam now wait to tell it gets worse, we will be scolded by the water and unable to breathe with the steam," he told her while starting a run. "You are going to wear yourself out running with me on your back!" she called out to him. "Trust me you will not be able to keep up," he told her, "By the way, you might want to keep your mouth shut or you'll bite your tongue. Just tap me if you see a place," he shouted out to her. Adieu did what she was told and kept a lookout, after a few moments the rain started coming down slightly harder to where the sand turned to steam. This kept the lost sand from coming up but it did make it slightly hard to see further. The heat from the water wasn't pleasant either and it took all Aduie had not to yell out in pain.

"I found us a placeholder on tight," Sha called out. Within a few moments both of them were under a rock caves shelter, and just in time for the rain became harder and scolding. "Are you alright?" he asked her while sliding her gently off his back. "I think so but what about you, your skin is red." Adieu pointed out to him. "I will be fine. I don't have that much clothing on so it did not hurt me that much. However, you are fully covered." he pointed out. Which was true and she did feel like she was still burning even after getting out of the rain. "Hold on I should have some dry clothes in my pack," Sha told her while digging around and then pulled out a dry cloak. "Here put this on and we will hang your clothes to dry," he told her while handing the cloak to her and then grabbing some rope out of his pack.

Adieu slid on the cloak first and then took the rest of her wet clothes off and handed them to him. She then watched as he took the rope and tied it on some sharp rocks and then hang the clothing on it. He then took the time to change his own clothing behind the already hung-up wet clothing. Though Adieu turned away and looked out to see lots of steam and hoped that Fang was alright. "I am sure your father is fine, exorcists are trained to withstand everything before being allowed to venture out. At least that's what many of them told me when they came to my village." Sai told her with a smile. Adieu wanted to smile back but she could not help but feel very uneasy. "Here we have something to eat and then get some rest, we have a day journey due to this rain. At least that's if it lets up," he told her while handing her some bread.

"Sorry it is not much but at least you won't go hungry," he told her. "It's fine thank you, you should rest too," she told him. "Trust me after you rest I will rest, I have more endurance than you do so go ahead," he told her though she was not sure if she took offense to his remark. Adieu decided to just let it slide due to the fact he was most likely right. She has never traveled before and was never able to do very much. "I wonder why rain is so hot? In Paragon it was always cold."Audie announced while taking the small roll from Sha.

"I have no clue, though, stand in it and you will be burned to death," he told her while sitting down against the cave wall. With no idea how long the rain would be Adieu sat watching the dessert while nibbling on the odd tasting roll in her hand. As the rain poured harder it was hard to hear anything else let alone see anything clearly if you had normal human eyes like Sha did, however, Adieu stared as if nothing was wrong and squirmed a bit when she saw what looked to be a wagon. Though she waited to say anything until she knew it for sure. "There is a wagon out there Sha, you don't think it's the slave traders again do you?" she asked her companion who just bared his teeth while looking outside. He was making plains from A to Z to keep his promise to get her to the iron gate as he promised.

"Sha that wagon is being attacked by demons!" she called out while darting out into the rain before Sai had any chance of grabbing her. "Get back here you will burn to death before you get to them!" he shouted at her. However, the rain was not so hot to her that she kept running to help the people who were in the wagon from those demons. Though she had no idea how she was going to do that, after all, she did not know much about the demons that were in this horrible world. As she got closer she could hear the screams of children and all she could think of was her life did not matter only they did.

Adieu grabbed hold of any demon she could and she heard them wail until they turned to ash. While doing this she had started enraging the lower demons to the point they started surrounding her from every angle. She had no time to think about herself when she heard the screams of the children inside the Wagon at this point the only thought was she had some sort of power like Sai's but would not hurt anyone that was in it. She looked around to see if there was a way she could make an opening to get to the kids but there was none. Adieu took the golden cross from her pocket and they started hissing. "God let this work cause I have nothing else up my sleeves," she mumbled underneath her breath. She charged right at the demons that were on her right and they backed away from her but not fast enough before they started burning around her.

"What the heck is going on?" she heard a man's voice yell out from where the children screamed. "If you guys have time to talk you have time to run. Now get out of here and head to the cave!" she yelled at them. "But there are so many," a woman called out and by this point, Adieu was getting annoyed. "Their gaze is upon me now, run for it!" she yelled out and this time she heard them running away. Some of the demons started noticing but she charged for them and was able to cut one of them with the cross and it screamed so loud that it made her ears ring and knocked her to the ground.

She watched as the black liquid poured out of the body of this demon as it screamed in agony. She watched in horror as this demon's blood started dissolving the demons around it and became a wall of dead flesh and bones only to see claws are out of it as if it was a door to their world. Fear froze over her as the Flesh Eater crawled out of it and came closer to her. She could feel her neck starting to burn once more but somehow she kept herself from passing out. "Get down!" Someone shouted and then pinned her to the ground. Within seconds the door of flesh started burning and the flesh-eater started hissing and sliding back into the pits of hell where it came from. The hot rain started coming down faster and the person that was on top of her refused to move while the fire was Blazing all around them. Adieu watched this demon going back into the whole.

She noticed something like a human body of a child being pulled in with it. She didn't know how but she shoved the man off of her and dashed towards the body. she grabbed the child and pulled their corps out of the Flesh- eaters claws. She felt her body starting to overheat but she did not give up. The demon's screams were unbearable and made her feel very dizzy and started getting dragged into the opening herself. As she started getting closer to the flames the hotter her body grew. She started gasping for breath while she dug her heels into the dirt to Anker herself.

"God if this keeps up I am going to die, But there is no way I am going to give up on this kid. They may be alive for all we know," Adieu grunted out to only where she could hear it. "Just let go girl if you don't you will die!" the man who pinned her down earlier called out. "I won't give up on them! Even if they are not alive they have the right to be buried where they can be remembered," she cried out. "God knows that body is not worth your life now let go!" the man yelled at her. Adieu felt the anger build in her chest as he kept repeating himself to let go to the point where her skin began to steam. "What the heck Girl what's going on with you?" the man questioned her. She could not answer for the pulsing in her ears kept her from hearing anything, her rage built up so much the flames around her became cold and did not hurt her anymore.

She looked at the hand of the demon and slammed her hand right on it and it burst into flames and yet the flames did not touch the child's body once. She pulled the child's body and herself out of the opening before it closed and the ground and the air were still on fire. After laying the child's body down she started calming down, though she knew that it was just a shell of one who used to live.

"Girl, what are you?" the man asked and she looked right at him. He wore the same uniform as her father Fang. "I am known as the devil's daughter from my village, though my father Fang said that it was not true." She told him. "I did not know Fang had a daughter," the man said, sounding so confused. "He adopted me a few days ago, though I just don't know how long it has been," she told him while her legs gave. "Well there is nothing saying he can't adopt a girl, but where is Fang?" the man asked. "I don't know I got separated from him while running away from the demons," she told him. "I am with Sai now and we are traveling to the Iron gate so I can meet up with Father Fang once again," she told him. "But girls are not allowed into the gates. Its men only." the man told her.

"I was told to wait for him by the fountain," she told him. "Oh, that is outside of the Iron gate church." the man told her. "Adieu! are you all right?" she heard Sai call out. Both of them looked to their right and the boy was running towards them. "Sai," she called out softly. "What happened?" he asked her while scooping her up in his arms. "There was a Flesh eater somehow I managed to cast it back into the pit of hell," Adieu told him and all he did was look at her in confusion. "Her body was in flames a moment ago," the man told him. "You are?" Sai asked him. "Oh yeah sorry my name is Father Markes. I am one of the elite Exorcists from the Iron Gate." the man told him. "Just the place we are trying to get to," Sai told him.

"Well, I can help you two get there, though I really can not say they would let her in. Though given the fact she is Fang's daughter they may overlook it," Markes told them though by the sound of his voice she knew it was a long shot. . "We will follow but I hope you understand that I will not trust you around her," Sai told him and Adieu couldn't help but wonder why. "I would be surprised if you did, by the way, child what is your name?" Markes asked her. "Adieu is my name, his is Sai," she told him in a weak voice while looking at the boy who held her. "Well, shall we make our way to that cave and get out of this rain?" Markes asked. "Yeah hold on," Sai told him and once more a bright light spun around them, but this time she did not feel a thing. "Odd," she mumbled out before dazing out in Sais's arms and he couldn't help but smile at the girl.

"That explains why this rain does not affect her like it does everything else," Sai whispered to himself not realizing that she heard him. "So are you Fang's son then?" Markes asked Sai as they walked back to the cave. "Never met the man, I am helping her because she saved my life. If I don't like this Father of hers I am not leaving her with him alone for one second." Sai informed the man but did not look at him, though he did not like or trust many people. Though with his barrier of wind he did not have to look around him for it was like a beacon for danger. *With that power that she has, I would not be surprised if she wasn't the devil's daughter. It is not natural and I am surprised that Fang even took her in,* Mark thought to himself.

All three went inside the cave where the family that Adieu saved huddled in fear. "Is it safe?" one of the girls asked. "For now yes, Sorry about one of your kids they did not make it," Sai told them and Adieu felt horrible for not getting there in time to save them. The woman in the group started crying and the father just stared at them. "Is she alright?" the same girl asked. "She just exhausted herself, with a bit of rest she will be good as new," Sai told her and the little girl gave out a small smile. "How could you hold that devil?" the man shouted and pointed to Adieu though she was already used to people being afraid of her. "This so-called devil you call her just saved your life and your family's!" Sai scolded him while laying her down on the ground and covered her in a blanket that was in his bag. "Before you go and judge her maybe you should thank her instead!" Sai continued which surprised her on hearing him so angry about it. Though no one said another word she could feel the rage filling the cave. "Just forget this man of fear, he will come around when he is no longer scared of the world," Markes told Sai.

"Fear or not this girl saved my life too, and if you had not noticed I also have powers and yet you don't call me a devil!" Sai pointed out and the man hung his head and just pulled his daughter and wife closer. *This boy may be a problem if the leader wants her killed,* Markes thought to himself. "If she is not a devil then what on earth is she?" Markes asked in a confused voice and she couldn't help but wonder that herself. "I don't know but God does give different types of gifts to everyone," Sai told him with a bit of irritation. *By the Mlooks of things that is her second gift, which means she will grow to the size she is meant to be.* Sai thought to himself as he remembered when he got his wind power.

"Well, this rain is going to last a few days so we all better just be kind to one another. I am going to put some demon wards up to keep them from getting in here." Markes told everyone and then took a glance right at Sai, "Looks like you need a rest, and keeping that barrier up is not going to help is it." Markes told him. "You are right about that but be warned of any funny business from anyone. I will not hesitate to hurt them," Sai warned while looking right at Markes. "No one is going to do anything. Though I wonder how big this cave is?" Markes told him. "Not sure, Why?" Sai asked. "Well, I just hope I have enough for all the entrances of this cave or at least the important areas," Markes informed him. Well just do enough for this area and then we will look around later," Sai told him.

"Good point. Well, it should not take too long," Markes told him. "Did you guys bring any stuff with you?" Sai asked the family. "All that we brought was damaged by those Demons, except my daughter's bear." the father told him. "Ok well, I have a little food but not enough to last us more than a couple of nights," Sai told them. "Please do not worry about us, we will be just fine. Take care of your sister and that's all," the wife spoke up after she was done sobbing so much. "Are you sure?" Sai asked her. "Yes, and watch that man who calls himself an exorcist I think he may be up to something," she warned him. "You don't trust him either ha," Sai couldn't help but smile while asking this question. "I have had a bad feeling since he had gotten into the wagon with us," she told him and that was the last thing Aduie heard before passing out.

CHAPTER ELEVEN
The six caverned cave

When Adieu woke back up she noticed that she was wrapped up in the blanket and in the sleeping Sai's lap. She tried to wiggle out but she knew she could not move without waking him up. She looked straight toward the opening of the Cave and it was still raining and the man who called himself Markes was sleeping next to it. She looked to her left and saw a different opening to the cave and on her right was the family of three she had saved. "Don't worry about what he said, they don't know you," She heard Sai softly tell her. "He is right though," Adieu told him. "If you are the devil's daughter then I am his son," Sai announced and she could not help but chuckle abet. Sai carefully sat up with her and placed her feet on the ground and unbundled her from the blanket. "You hungry?" he asked her. "Yeah but first I need to pee," she announced and all he did was look around. "You may be able to do that there, though we have not checked the place yet," Sai told her.

"I will go check it out," she told him while walking over to the opening and saw strange papers everywhere on the opening. *Thoughts must be the warders,* she thought to herself and carefully placed a finger on the paper but nothing happened. She gave a small sigh of relief and then stuck her hand through the opening and pulled it back and again nothing happened. "High Sai, if I can't get back in can you do something about it?" Adieu asked. "It won't do anything to you," she heard Markes tell her. "If it doesn't make you sick or make you want to run you are safe from it," Markes told her. "Then that means you are not the Devil's daughter then," Sai told her with a smile. "No, it means I am not a demon. You forget the

Devil was an angel first." Adieu told him while walking through. "She has a point," Markes announced in a big echoing voice which woke up the family.

"Yes I will do something about it," Sai told her and she went inside the other entrance. "Does anyone have a light of some sort?" She called out when it was too dark to see. "Yeah hold on," Sai told her and then handed her a small Lantern with a candle. "Thanks, she called out and while she was staring at cave walls around her she could hear the little girl talking to her mom saying that she was hungry and had to use a bathroom. The mother was trying to console her daughter that they would find something to eat and that I was looking for a bathroom as they spoke. The cave was divided into what looked like four caverns, two on her left and two on her right. She decided to go left and take the cavern on the right. There she found platforms with medium size holes in them she noticed that there were old candles stuck by old candle wax in the walls high enough where no one would get burned. She looked around and saw nothing dangerous in the holes of the rocks and when she dropped a pebble in the four holes it took a while for them to hit the ground. Very quickly she pulled down her pants and sat on the rock and went to the bathroom.

To her surprise, it was very smooth and after she was done she quickly lit the old candles and then went to tell the others what she found. While everyone else was using the bathroom she went and explored the cave next to it. from there she noticed more old candles and lit them there she saw places where people slept at some point. some of their bags were still there, and when she looked at them closely they were old and ripped. "You guys don't think we are in someone's home do you?" she heard Markets voice echo all around. "I don't think they live here anymore," she heard Sai call out. "The second cave on the right looks to be a graveyard and there is an old skeleton on the ground," She heard Sai call out. With that, she looked through the old bags and mumbled to herself for their souls to forgive her trespassing.

She did not find anything that would be considered food but she did find more candles and an old journal that had faded out. "We should bury him and make a gravestone for the little girl too," Adieu called out to them. "So this is where you were, what did you find?" Sai asked. "Candles and a book that we should bury with the body," she told him. "I don't know if we have any tools to do that right now. Though there has to be a shovel somewhere for the others to be buried," Sai told her. "You are most likely right, though he also could have brought the dirt from outside to do it." Adieu pointed out to him.``You could be right on that given that it's all rock and no dirt," he told her. "What was in the one next to it?" she asked him. It looked to be a storage area but there was not enough light for it." he told her. "Too bad, there was nowhere to take a bath," she told him and all he could do was laugh. "Once we get to the Iron gate I am sure we can get a bath," he told her. Should we go check out the storage area?" she asked him.

"Wouldn't hurt, but I feel like doing that would be in the wrong somehow," he told her. "In a way, it is, however, if we are correct in knowing everyone is dead here then we are not stealing and we do need to survive somehow. The worst thing we could do is just organize everything if anyone still lives here." Adieu told him. Knowing that she made a valid point made him feel a little better about it. Both got up and went to the cave on the right side and looked through it, all it was was old wooden barrels and crates that had nothing in them. The shelves were old and weathered that they cracked and crashed to the floor kicking up dust all around them. Both started coughing as they ran for the opening and went back to the start of the cave. "You two alright?" Markes asked, handing them a cantine. "Yea... just..lo..looking ... at. the .. storage room to see if there was more food or not," Adieu told him while coughing her head off. "Any luck?" the father asked in a low voice, and by the looks of him and the mother, they had been crying all night. "No, sorry," Adieu told her while looking at the floor.

"It's not your fault Dear, none of it is." the woman told her, and when she looked at the woman she had no hatred in her eyes. "It does look like it would be a good home outside of the home for anyone traveling. though it looks like whoever lived here did not take demons and the rain into consideration." Markes announced. "But at least we know there is only one entrance to this cave at least for now," Sai informed everyone. "Yes but there are seven of us, we have no idea how long the rain is going to last and there is no food for everyone here," Markes announced. "My wife and I use to not eating for a while, if anyone could make sure our daughter has little to eat we would be grateful." the man announced. "I will make sure she gets something, I do not have a lot but between Adieu and her, it should last," Sai told them.

"How about you exorcist?" Sai asked him. "We go through a month of training with no food. I can last a while without food myself," Markes told him and both Adieu and Sai could not help but wonder then why he pointed it out that there were seven of them. Just by the look of Sai's eyes, Adieu knew he did not trust him either, though for now to give him the benefit of the doubt. "You said your name was Markes right?" Adieu asked him without a single note in her voice. "Yes, is there something you need?" he asked her. "No, not really. I was just wondering if you ran into my father at any point while in your travels?" she asked him. "No, I have not seen Fang in many months now, to be honest, to meet another Exorcist while on missions are not really normal unless both are going home at the same time," Markes told her. "How many of you are there?" she asked. "Well, the last time I heard a number was ten of us at least. though there are many that train to become one. though the training is very tuff and many die trying. We are lucky if one makes it every twenty years." Markes told her.

"What kind of training do you go through?" Adieu asked him. "That is a secret only known to us, and the one who died in training," Markes told her. Without his knowledge, she was reasoning to every note in his voice and within those notes, she heard hissing than words themselves. *I don't trust him, there is darkness in his soul,* she thought to herself though she was a bit surprised to even think that. "Adieu will you come with me?" she heard Sai ask her and she took her gaze off the man dressed in black and turned to face her new companion. He turned back to the other entrance and started walking away and she followed his footsteps. He walked into where the bathroom was and she couldn't help but wonder why but did not ask. He stood in the middle of the room looking around and then walked to his left and just started looking carefully around the walls. "What's wrong Sai?" she finally asked him.

"Nothing, I don't want you near him without me by your side," he told her while examining the walls. "Are you thinking he is a bad man or that he is hiding something?" she asked him. "I am not sure yet, I try not to judge people too soon. Though that does not mean I trust than either," he told her. "That is a commendable trait," she told him as she watched him. "What are you looking for?" she asked him after a while of watching him. "I am looking for tabernacles," he told her, and then when she gave him a weird look he just smiled. "How do you find these tabanackels?" she asked him which made him laugh a bit. "Tab.er.nak.els" he slowly pronounced to her. "Yeah those, how do you find them?" she asked him, a bit embarrassed about her mistake. "Normally there is a secret way to open them. A form of a button or a lever," he told her.

Adieu watched this boy tap on the walls for a few seconds and then looked around herself. She relit the lantern that Sai gave her earlier that morning with one of the old candles and then walked around the area. Though there was nothing but walls and even though she checked the walls for any openings like she saw Sai doing so nothing showed up. After the bathroom, they went to the dust storage room and shuffled through the mess. "Why would anyone pick this place to live in?" Adieu asked the boy she was with.

"This place would be free, there in the middle of every town. To be honest there are many different reasons that someone would pick this place." Sai told her. "You need money for a lot of things don't you?" Adieu asked him and Sai stopped clearing the broken wood and stared at her. "Adieu did your father teach you anything?" he asked her. "Some things on demons, but that was a few days ago why?" she asked him. "You said he adopted you right?" he asked. "Yes I lived on the street since I was very little, in a small town called Virgoous," she told him.

"I see but you should have learned some stuff while living on your own right?" Sai asked her. "I guess but not sure what all I really learned," she told him and all he did was just look at her in disbelief. "So why do you call yourself the Devil's daughter?" Sai asked her. "That's what the village called me, " she told him. "Why?" he asked her. "Can you keep a secret?" she asked. "Yeah," he told her and she pulled off the Black ribbon on her neck. The three puncture wounds hardly showed until she held the candle next to her neck. "You were bitten," he said quietly as he came closer to her and placed his hand over it. "I was told that I got them when my parents died," she told him as she put the ribbon with the silver moon on it back on.

"I'm sorry," he told her after a few seconds after hearing about her parents. "I am guessing the village knew it was a demon that bit you that's why they were too scared of you," he told her. "I am not sure if they were scared but I was never allowed inside any homes or buildings," she told him.

"So everything has been new for you then?" Sai asked. "Yeah, but it has been fun and terrifying at the same time," she told him with a small smile. After that, they continued cleaning the storage room in silence. Once they were done both looked for secret rooms but found none, Adieu figured it was to pass the time while they were stuck. After a while, they went back into the room with everyone else and had something small to eat and then curled next to a wall and fell asleep.

Though Adieu's sleep was not long, she heard something moving in the back room, though when she looked everyone was together. She got up and lit the lantern once more and headed to the back. there she saw nothing in the back room and went to the storage room and saw nothing, she then went to the room that had the body and still nothing but she felt a presence that was not very calming. She didn't have enough time to turn around when something grabbed her and pulled her backward making her let out a scream in the darkness.

CHAPTER TWELVE
The Blood Hotspring

When she hit the cave wall the lantern fell from her hand and crashed to the floor engulfing the cavern into flames. Though the flames did not harm her as they burned her clothing. "What's going on?" she cried out while looking around for a way out. "It's useless," a formulaic voice warned her from behind. When she turned around there was no one around. "You're the shadow are you not?" Adieu called out to it and it only laughed. "Why are you doing this?" she asked. "I am not doing anything, you are," it told her. "What do you mean?" she asked ``you're trying to wake but your true self is so dormant that it is out of control." the voice told her.

"What do you mean?" she asked. "You have so much hate and hurt within your soul that it's trying to escape but you won't let it." the shadow told her. She felt arms wrap around her body and yet they could not be seen. Then my village was right. I am a monster?" she asked while feeling her body go numb but she did not fall. "Your so-called village is ignorant fouls." The shadow told her. "You could have protected them if they were not full of hate for what they never understood. I can help you rise to your heights if you allow me to." the shadow told her. "I don't want to hurt anyone," Adieu said. "But you have already killed so many, and they all deserved it." the shadow told her. "What do you mean?" she asked. "All will be revealed in time child , now close your eyes," the Shadow told her, and without meaning to, she closed her eyes.

She could hear screaming all around her and men shouting, none of the voices she could make out. All was darkness and chaotic, "Who's screaming?" she heard herself whisper. "All souls that will be in total damnation for the hell they put others in." the shadow told her. "All of these are people that have died?" she asked and when she opened her eyes she saw bones covering the cave floor and ghost-like figures were chained by the flames that surrounded them. None of these people she knew and yet her heart ached for them.

Though the heat was so strong that she could not even cry one tear for them. "How do I get out of here?" she asked while putting her left hand over her heart and clenched it. "Let your power lead you," the shadow told her. With that, she felt her body fall down a long dark hole where the screams became worse but the only thing she could feel was something cold and heavy holding her body. She couldn't even speak when laughter felled her ears as something snakes wrapped themselves around her body from feet to chest. She felt teeth sink into her neck and claws go down her back. She could feel warm liquid running down her back and dripping into something below her. She felt her life starting to fade away as the sounds of the screaming vanished without a trace.

"Now let's get rid of this fake image," she heard someone hiss out and someone agreeing in a darker sinister voice. She could not make a single sound as she felt her body being ripped apart and bones snapping. She couldn't even think straight. The only thing she could do is fear death was closing in on her faster than she had hoped. "Silly child you're not going to die, at least not yet," the sinister voice laughed out while gouging out her face. After they were done the snakes let her go and she fell hard to the floor and splashed in a pool of her own blood. All the pain came to her all at once and she let out such a scream that would turn your hair white as a ghost. She heard something banging against something but she could not figure out where it was coming from. She was drowning in her own blood not sure if she would ever see the man who gave her a new life ever again or see the boy who became her companion. "You are now reborn in the blood of your father and your mother," the shadow told her. "Pull yourself out and you will have the life meant for you right away." the shadow told her. Though she could hardly move through the pain she could feel her lungs filling up with the blood covering her whole body.

Which way do I go to get out of here? she thought to herself. She managed to move her right arm and felt something hit her fingertips. As quickly as she could she clawed her way up and over the pool and fell onto the cave floor. She then felt someone grab her and shake her, and could hear someone calling her name. She heard her own voice telling this person she didn't want to die before a sharp pain struck her right cheek. "Is she all right?" she heard a woman ask. "I don't know she is so cold." a boy's voice came into play. "Well at least she is breathing again, but where the hell did that tub come from?" another man's voice asked. "I don't know it was not here when any of us was in here before," the woman's voice became a bit louder. "Adieu please open your eyes," the boy's voice asked while shaking her a couple of times. "What the hell got a hold of her, I mean look at her back." the man's voice piped up.

"Beats me, so much for your damn fucked up charms right," the boy yelled at the man. "They work on demons whatever grabbed her was no demon," Aduie heard the man explained. "It was a shadow figure," she managed to get out while gasping for air. She felt her body shaking as if there was an earthquake had hit. "What are you talking about?" Sai asked her while trying to gather the shacking girl in his arms. "So much screaming, so much pain, I don't want to see it anymore." she managed to get out while her eyes watered up. "What are you talking about?" Markes's voice chimed in. "Poor dear she must have had a really bad nightmare," the woman announced while wrapping the shaking girl in a blanket. "Let's get her out of here, when she fully wakes up we can ask her all about it," Markes told everyone.

"I think we should leave it alone until she is ready to tell us herself," Sai told them while managing to get the shaking girl in his arms and took her to the other room where the father and little girl were. "What happened?" the father asked them. "We are not sure but don't go into the bathroom area tomorrow until I have a chance to take a look." Markes's voice bounced off the walls. "I think that is a good idea," the woman told them. "Whatever happened it's a mess in there," Sai warned them. "Is she ok?" the little girl asked. "There does not seem to be any injuries but whatever happened to her scared her really badly. Her hair is turning white," Sai announced as Adieu clenched his arm. "She drew blood," the father pointed out.

"It's all right, it will heal quickly anyway," Sai told them. "Lineal right?" he asked the man who said yes. "Can you light me that two lanterns and with Markes plant them in the storage room on the far left back corner and right next to the door on the right side?" Sai asked him. "Yes but why?" he asked. "I am going to do a purification to make this place safer," Sai told him. While picking her back up. Adieu heard the men rushing around and in a few moments, they came back and told him it was done. "Do you want me to pray over this place?" Markes asked them. "No, What I am about to do will be strong enough," Sai told him. Adieu looked right at him and all he did was smile and mouth it will be alright.

Both entered the Storage rooms and she heard the boy telling them to stay in the other room and don't come running if they hear anything. They all agreed and the father told him he would hold his daughter to prevent her from running to them. Sai waited until no one was around or close to the other door before he started. A light Resonated so brightly over him as he started mumbling something in a different Language. It filled the whole cavern. Adieu felt herself calming down and her body stopped shaking and became limp.

Though this time she was not scared but peaceful for the first time in her life. She did not know the language that he was speaking but she saw the blood that was seeping out of her nail marks on him disappear and the wound healed so fast.

All the pain that filled her slowly faded and her heart slowed down its pace to the point it was beating normally. Her throat was no longer dry and felt closed off that she was able to breathe slowly once again. She looked around in all and every color from the walls turned bright and almost polished looking. She felt the puffiness of her eyes from crying and her tears fade away from her face. "What's going on?" she whispered while she watched the lantern in the far back blow out. She looked into Sais's eyes and they had a golden glow to them. she saw him smile as he was repeating the same word over and over again. There was a small amount of smokiness to the air but there was a smell of Lavender as well that kept her calm and collected.

When the Lavender smell filled the air She could feel different presents that had a strong evil feel to them and when she went to take a look he cuffed her face with his hands and just had her look at him. There were brutal blood-curdling screams and hissing all around them but somehow she stayed calm. The smell changed into rosemary and she could hear something dark speaking the same language but saying something different. The screams became more intense and she could hear a woman crying for someone not to take her child away from her. Adieu wanted to look but Sai shook his head no and kept her locked on him. Though the voice sounded so familiar to her, but not at the same time. The woman's voice became Horsted and very wicked quickly and started cursing them and screamed in pain.

For Adieu this went on for hours and even though this was going on Sai kept her calm until the light vanished and all the sounds vanished and all went quiet. "There that should do it," he whispered and sat down with his back at the wall. "What was that?" Adieu asked while he let go of her. "I drove all the evil out of here I think, though it was tough," he told her. "How do you feel?" he asked her. "I'm ok," she told him. "Good, I'm glad," he told her while closing his eyes. Adieu sat down next to him as the room became dark once more and clung to his arm.

"You going to make it?" Adieu asked him in a slight quiet voice. "Yeah just need a moment, but thank you for not fighting me too much on trying to look," he told her. "I figured you had a reason but what happened?" she asked him. "It's called purifying. it is not easy to do and when people look at what I am driving out they either will be dragged into the pits of hell, or killed on the spot. Either way, it is not pleasant." he explained to her. "What are you?" she asked him and all he could do was smile. "I guess that will be determined someday. maybe the same as you," he told her. "Adieu doubted it; however he could be this so-called God's Son. "Are the others ok?" she asked. Well if they lessoned to me then yes, if not then no," he told her.

"Is everyone all right she called out and did not respond. "Well, that either means that they are not sure if it's done, or they were stupid," Sai told her while getting up. "I don't have a candle," she told him. "I don't either but we should be fine," Sai told her and took her hand and started leading her out of the storage room and back into the entrance Where they found everyone with their eyes closed. "It's all done now you guys we should be safe for now," Sai told everyone and then collapsed to the ground. "Poor dear he must have had it ruff," the lady cried out. "Hold on kid we got him," Markes told Adieu before she tried to pick him up or anything.

Adieu watched him with every second that they had left in the cave while it continued to rain. The woman helped her by bringing in water from the rain and placing a cloth on his head. Surprisingly once the water entered the cave it became cool to use. "Stupid fool used all his strength when it would have only taken me just a few papers to make it safe," Markes announced after the third day that he was unconscious. "If you could have done that you should have done it while putting up the demon barrier!" Adieu yelled at him without even looking at him. "You think that I run into evil spirits that often girl? the main thing we are taught is guarding against demons, not spirits!" Markes pointed out. "Well then don't bost that you could have done it with pieces of paper when you didn't even think about it after seeing a dead body in the grave room," Adieu told him.

"Even though there were not many times that she heard it, she always hated people that say they could have done something but chose not to or lied about knowing how to do it. "Well, he is not going to be up any time soon so I am going into the bathroom to check it out," Markes told everyone. "The boy told us no to go in," the woman told him. "I am an Exorcist. I know how to take care of myself and others," Markes sneered. "I will go in with you," Adieu told him and all he did was look at her. "I have things to look at too, and that is all," Adieu told him while wondering about the images she saw and the feeling of her skin was ripped off her body. "Fine, but don't get in my way," Markes told her.

CHAPTER THIRTEEN
Darkened Path

Both entered the darkroom with their lanterns Markes went in all the way as Adieu stood in the doorway while Markes lit the rest of the candles. Once the room was bright she walked all the way in as well. Adieu saw a giant hole in the far left wall where it was pitch black and had a very metallic smell to it. "What is that smell?" she asked him. "That would be the smell of blood, by the way, it smells it's fresh and old at the same time," Markes told her. She watched him enter the hole and look around for a moment before going in herself. "Is there a hole in the ground or maybe a tub that's filled with anything?" she asked while looking to her left and then her right. "Yeah there is a tub here, and by the looks of it looks like blood," he told her. "How deep do you think it could be?" She asked him.

"It should be arm's length," he told her and then looked at her like she was weird. "Ok so I should not drown in that right?" she asked him. "You're not going swimming , are you?" he asked her. "I have to check the bottom," she told him and he just looked from her to the tub back to her. "Why?" he asked her after a moment. "I need to check to see if there is human skin in there," she told him. "OK, you are one weird chick," he told her as he took off his coat and shirt. He then reached in and pulled a bunch of skin and hair out of the tub. "How the fuck did you know that it was in here?" Markes asked her and all she could do was look at it all she could do was look right at it in horror.

"Well, girl? how did you know it was there?" Markes asked once again but this time more aggression was in his voice. "I have to go," Adieu told him and ran out of the cavern and right out into the rain. she did not look back even when the woman was shouting for her to come back. The only thought that ran through her head was she had to get away from them before she did any harm to them. She just looked ahead of her as she ran for it. She did not know where to go but she knew that meeting up with Fang was no longer an option for her. *I am a demon, it was no lie that my village told me.* she thought to herself as some tears formed in her eyes making things a little blurry.

Once again demons surrounded her and snarled at one another for getting too close to each other. "There is no way that I couldn't be, my skin was ripped off and yet I have it on me. Is the Devil a Flesh Eater?" she asked herself while still running and was not watching where she was going and tripped. This left her an easy target and three demon canine dogs launched at her but disintegrated. "But why the demons attack me and why do they die if they touch me?" she asked while watching all that attacked her turned to dust before her eyes. Even though they turned to dust they did leave scratches on her skin.

The ashes of the demons seeped into the scratches that they left her and they started to burn though this did not bother her too much at first with all the ash that was coming down it became unbearable. She had no idea what to do next nor why she thought running off in a desert was a good idea. She knew being away from them would be the best Idea though she did not calm down fast enough to think it through. "What do I do know, I don't even know how I did those flames," she told herself. "Stay down!" she heard someone yell out and something splashed her and made all the demons burn into nothing. "That was close are you alright?" the voice asked her. She smelled her clothing but nothing was odd about the liquid.

"Oh sorry about getting you wet, don't worry it's just holy water." Then voice told her as it held out a hand. When she looked up it was a young boy. "Hi Father Leo there's a cute girl over here!" he yelled out. "Sorry that was loud, my name is John, you're not hurt are you.?" the boy asked without a breath as he helped her up. "Oh no you're all scratched up," he announced then again once again he yelled in her ear for this Father Leo.

"John doesn't yell in that poor girl's ear, and if she is hurt use what I taught you," a man's voice scolded him while coming closer to them.

When he came into view he had reddish hair, dressed in full black, and had a silver cross on his shirt. The boy had brown hair and freckles and wore green clothing. "Oh my, you are a young girl. Let's take a look at those scratches." the Man told her while kneeling down to her level.

"They are not too deep and there does not seem to be any poison in your wounds from the ash." the man told her. "Are you an Exorcist like Father Fang, and Markes?" Adieu asked him. "Yes, so you had a run-in with those two ha. I am not surprised but at the same time not many people meat more than two of us." the man told her. "Father Fang adopted me, and the one called Markes is in a nearby cave," she informed him. "Oh, I see. well then is Father Fang there too?" he asked. "No, I got split up from him a while back.

I am with a boy that helped me escape from Slave collectors," she told him. "Then why is he not with you?" the man asked. "I ran off without thinking things through," she told him. "Well, my dear that is never a good thing, however, you did not go that far. Let's get you back to the cave and there we will rest up abet before continuing to our destination." Father Leo told her. "But... all right let's go," she told him while they started walking, though every bone in her body screamed to run away again. When she entered the cave again she was grabbed so fast and held for a second. "Thank God you are back, are you hurt?" Sai's voice rang so loudly in her ears. "A few scratches, nothing more," Leo answered him.

"Good, now my next question, what the hell were you thinking running off like that!" he yelled at her. "Now hold on, let her set down and get some water, I am sure she will tell you everything when the time comes. It is natural for one to get scared or angry and run off without telling anyone," Leo told him while stepping in front of both of them. "Father Leon, the pacifist when it comes to humans," Markes teased. "Oh yes, she warned me that the Dark Exorcist was here too. Now, why do I think you were the reason this girl ran away from here?" Father Leo exclaimed.

"It wasn't him," Adieu spoke up and both men looked surprised to hear it. "Then why?" Sai asked. "It must have something to do with the skin that was in that tub, somehow she knew it was there. When I asked her about it she freaked." Markes informed everyone about it. "Then why did you not go after her?" Sai asked. "I am still human, and unlike her, I can be harmed by the scorched rain." Markes pointed out. "I forgot for some reason you can't cast a barrier around your skin." Father Leo sighed out. "By the way, what was up with that skin that freaked you out so badly?" Markes asked her.

"I was dragged into that room and plunged into that tub. I couldn't move. It was like I was chained up. At that same time, I could feel my skin being ripped off of my body. When I saw the skin I..." Adieu started telling them but just couldn't finish saying the last few words. "Dang kid, you know all you had to do was just tell me that to begin with. That skin is old skin. It was preserved by the liquid that it was in. I get your freak out though given the fact you have powers that no one else does. Plus what this boy told us you've been called a demon all your life. So naturally, you would start thinking you were one after that." Markes pointed out.

"Why did you go in there in the first place after I told you guys not to?" Sai asked her and all she could do was look at him. "Well, the thing is, she probably did not trust me to go back there by myself. You don't trust me either so why would she trust me, after all, you two are siblings are you not?" Markes pointed out. Neither of them really said anything nor did Adieu really think that to begin with though she did like the thought of having a brother and a father.

"Oh and don't worry I will personally send someone From the Irongates to come and destroy this lab of evil," Markes announced. "Don't destroy it, just get the blood out of this place and people can use it as a safe haven through the desert, Besides the way I cleansed it no one can use this place for evil deeds. Though holey ritual can make a great wave using this place," Sai told them. "Your right it does have a much holy ground feel to it," Father Leo told him. "It should after all it took everything I had to make this place safe. Though if he had put up papers I would not have been able to do any of it." Sai told him.

"Well I know you guys have been waiting for the rain to stop but please hang out for a little while longer," Father Leo told all of them. "Sure, besides I can't leave until she is fully rested." Father Markes told him. "In that case Where are you heading to Markes?" Leo asked him. "I am on my way home, these two will be tagging along. Though I really don't think her being Father Fangs Adopted daughter will mean anything to them." Markes announced. "It most likely won't, however, Fang would not have sent her there if he didn't think they wouldn't." Father Leo told him. "Speaking of Fang have you seen him on your travels?" Sai asked him. "As I told the girl No, I wish I did to give you guys some ease." Father Leo told them. "Though watch him fight, Father Fang can take care of himself," John told them with a very happy face. "Well Leon, where are you and the brat going?" Markes asked. "We are off to Virgoous to take care of something leaving bones of children in their house." Father Leo told him.

"Virgoous? That is the village I just came from there with Father Fang. The MAyor's daughter was killed the night before Father Fang adopted me. I remember it because I saw Greyish demons with glowing red eyes. Those are the only thing that I saw last night except a shadow figure sharing my box." she told them. "A shadow figure? did it talk to you?" Leo asks her. "Yes, it informed me that those types of demons are attracted by fear. Oh and that he would not let them hurt me, that is about it I believe," she informed them. "Is there anything else you can remember about that night?" Father Leo asked her. "No, I passed out after a while. Though I think I smelled smoke from a cigar," she told them.

"I see, is there anything you can remember from the morning?" Leo asked her. "Yes everyone went to the town hall, and the bones were a skull and two arm bones were shown. After that Fang took me in got me into a room and told me to bathe. During my bath, a Flesh eater appeared into the room and came after me. I dashed out of the tub and head in between the bed and the wall. I then saw it shed its skin and disappear. After that Fang came back got pissed off and yelled at the doctor. That's when he told me I was now his daughter." she told him. "That flesh-eater must have just eaten enough to evolve," Markes told her. "I have no idea, but I lived out in the streets for years and I never saw a demon before. Why that night?" Adieu asked. "I don't know however if I get any info I will let you know what's up," Leo told her. "Thank you," Adieu told him. "Of course that is as long the elder does not silence you," Markes told him. "I don't have to tell him how I got the info," Leo told him.

"That and he doesn't need to know that I told her anything," Father Leo told him. Markes just shook his head, Adieu and Sai just watched as these men acted like siblings themselves. "Well, then how are you feeling kid?" Markes asked her. "I feel like I am starving," she told them once she gave herself time to think and within seconds her stomach growled and everyone laughed. "Well dear you haven't eaten a single bite since he was asleep for two days," the woman informed her. "You did what? Why?" Sai asked, scolding her for a second time that day. Adieu was not used to this at all and it made her feel weirdly upset and happy at the same time. "Don't be too mad at her Dear, a woman does that when she is worried about people they care about. It is quite normal." the woman told him. "She is not kidding, when Lizzy fell sick Mitsy refused to leave her side and did not eat till she was better. Though by then Mitzy was sick herself," the man called Linal told them.

"That won't do, if that happens again you need to eat and take care of yourself," Sai told her. "I will try," she told him though she didn't know if she would or not. "Well you people are in luck, We have plenty of food with us," Leo told them and John slammed his bag on the ground. "Anyone not a meat eater?" John called out and everyone just looked at him. "If everyone pitches in we should be able to have a good meal," Father Leo told everyone while pulling a bucket out of his own bag and a few twigs and made a cauldron. Everyone had their jobs. Mitzy cleaned the dishes to eat out of, Markes and Linal grabbed the wood, Sai grabbed some burnt-up clothing and lit the fire. Adieu watched little Lizzy while the grown-ups worked on their meal. When the smell filled the entrance of the cave her stomach started cramping. "Hi take some bread, it should tie you over before all of it is done," Sai told her and by his facial expression, she could tell he was worried.

"I'll be fine," she told him with a smile. She was used to going hungry for a while unless a stranger took pity on her and gave her food. Though she was wondering what she would have to do this time to be able to eat. "You sure?" Sai asked her. "Yeah, but what job do I need to do?" she asked and they just looked at her. "What do you mean?" Father Leo asked her. "Well in Virgoous when strangers gave me food I took the luggage to their rooms or showed them around town. When Sai and I were in another town I washed floors," she told them. "Oh my, Dear they didn't make you do anything else did they?" Mitzy asked her and Adieu just stared at her a bit confused. "By the sounds of things you have had it ruff, however, you already gave me something that I needed, so I will take the information you gave me as payment for the food." Father Leo told her and she was very puzzled.

"Hi is there anything else about the town itself you can tell us?" John asked her. "Well, the Mayor's family area a huge deal for their family founded the town. To my knowledge, everyone in the town loves them, though I do know some of the young girls did not like the daughter so much due to the fact she was not really nice to anyone her age," Adieu told them in between bites of her bread. "The town is small and the biggest attraction is the bell tower made by the first group of people that lived there. it is very dusty and something in the earth will not allow anything to grow. That is all I really know," she told them. "Well, when I am there I will check the soil and see if there is anything we can do about that." Father Leo told her.

Once the soup was ready everyone chowed down and for once Aduie had seconds of everything. No one really talked while eating but as soon as they were done Mitzy barked orders to everyone for clean up. Though for some reason she told Adieu to just sit and relax that the men would take care of it. Once everything was cleaned up from the meal, everyone packed up their stuff and was ready to head out the next day. Father Leo and Markes gave charms to the family to protect them from demons in their travels. Adieu checked her own bag that she had forgotten when she ran off to see if Fang's gold cross was still in it. "Oh wow, I am surprised Fang gave you a gold cross. Father Leo, I thought gold was to attract evil, if that is the case why would he give that to her?" John asked. "That would be a question to ask Father Fang, though I am sure this young woman could give you that answer if you ask her." Father Leo told him. "For some reason, I am able to use it to defend myself against demons so he told me to keep it on me," she told them as she put it back in the bag.

"It looks all scratched up," John told her. "Well it's been through hell and back many times, and to be used in a fight well of course it would get damaged a bit. However, I am sure the blacksmith with be willing to fix it up for you." Father Leo told her. "Oh, you are going to need this, I know girls are not allowed in but with that gold cross from Father fang you just need three more things without him," he told her while going through his own bag. He proceeds to pull out a slip of paper and hands it to her. "It's a letter of recommendation to the Iron church," Father Leo told her. "What's the third thing?" Sai asked him. "That would be an escort and that would follow with being with me. Since you are a man you won't need one, but if they will let her past the gate then she will need that letter and an escort. Also since she has one of Father Fang's crosses with his seal on it then they know she is highly recommended." Markes told them. "I see, I will still be able to keep her company correct?" Sai asked him.

CHAPTER FOURTEEN
Kahoy Village

"How long until we get there?" Sai asked Markes. "Should be three more days unless we run into any more trouble," Markes told him. "Hope not, I am done with those damn things," Sai told him while looking back at Adieu who was just walking as fast as she could. "You really should watch your mouth around a girl," Markes scolded him. "Yeah well I am sure she has heard much worse, plus I am not going to change the way I talk for anyone," Sai told him and Adieu could not help but laugh. "Just don't follow that mouth of his, Fang would get very mad at you," Markes warned her. "As much as I appreciate your warnings, I am sure he has cursed himself," Adieu told him while still smiling. "I can already tell you will fit right into the Iron academy if they let you in," Markes told her. "Well if they don't then we will just have to find another way to get her back with this Father Fang," Sai told him.

"No doubt that you would, knowing Fang he would give up the Exorcist title to take care of her too. Fang does not take anyone in so he sees something in her." Markes told them. "We do not have any camping gear so it is going to be a cold night," Sai announced. "What on earth are you talking about kid, we will be reaching Kohay soon we will get a hotel there. I know you guys don't have any money so just let me do the talking and we will be all set." Markes told them. "Please tell me you are not going to scam these people," Sai protested. "How dare you, I am an Exorcist you two are with me. I have certain strings in most of the villages." Markes informed him. "They are that important?" Adieu couldn't help but ask while trying not to lose balance in the sand. "Yes, we are almost like royalty." Markes bosted.

"So you guys have more fucked up ego to go around do you?" Sai asked him. "Sai, he is being nice and helping us out. Do you think you could try and not piss him off?" Adieu asked her companion. "Fine, but if you guys are such a big deal why are there only ten of you?" Sai asked. "The training is very difficult and not everyone makes it. Their power depletes or their physical being can't handle their power getting stronger and they die. Everyone is told this before they start any of it, and then you have those who give up after a few days of it." Markes told them. "I see why women are not allowed?" Adieu asked while catching her balance. "Gee kid where did you learn how to walk? And to answer your question yes and no. Most women don't process the spiritual needs to be an Exorcist. Also, giving the fact that there are not a lot of women in every village so keeping them safe and not put them in the battle with demons that will rip them apart without a second thought." Markes told them.

"Where do these demons come from anyway?" Adieu asked him. "Well the leader says they come from the depths of hell, however, there are some that say they are made from the greedy desires of men. So to be honest no one really knows where they come from." Markes told her. "So you are saying there is no end to this job so you guys have it made." Sai pointed out. "We don't get paid a lot if that's what you are asking, though when we do get paid it's enough to get us by. We also have to put half of what we get into the Exorcist share account. That is to help buy food and things that the whole team needs to survive. Though there have been times where you can get something for yourself instead." Markes told them.

"So the Kohoy Village, what are we looking at there?" Sai asked. "Well, it's one of the wealthy places that most rich people live. Good food, electricity and hot water, and the softest bed you have ever laid your body on. To be honest it's like your sleeping on air or water if you like water beds. Though you have to be on your best behavior and cursing is not allowed in there." Markes told them. "Well sounds like a place that is asking for trouble," Sai told him. "Will yes, though we have made sure that demons can't get in, though we have to come by and check on them every three years to make sure they are still intact," Markes told them. "So how much do these guys pay you to do all this," Sai asked. "Will they be where we get the most money for the whole clan to stay alive," Markes told them. "Great so they are bigger-than-life people, I may just sleep out in the desert," Sai announced while they came to a gate.

"Wow it's already been half a day," Adieu announced. "Yes, by the time we get to the other village it would be nightfall tomorrow. That's why we are stopping here now before continuing so we don't get trapped out there during the night," Markes told them while approaching a marble gate. "Yo Markes what's up my man, how's it digging?" a strange man called out as the marble gate opened behind him. "Gusto Levi, My man you have not changed a bit since the last time I saw you, three years ago. Tell me any trouble?" Markes asked. "No man has ever been chill of late. Though Markes who are these kids with you?" the man asked him. "Oh God, nope I will sleep out here tonight I can't take that talk at all," Sai complained. "This rude boy is Sai and this cute kid is Aduie and she is the daughter of the one and only Father Fang," Markes told him.

"Well come in my man, and you two I was told that it will be training fire tonight my man." the man told everyone. "What do you mean it is going to rain fire?" Sai asked. "The sun did feel a bit hotter today," Aduie told them. "Perhaps the stairs are going to be falling tonight," she finished before Sai was able to ask her what she was talking about. "You are almost right, they will be comments that will be falling. This has happened before in the days of God's judgment days and it will happen again before the end of days," Markes told her. "What the hell are you talking about?" Sai asked him while watching Markes walk through the gate. "Come on Sai, I really need a bath," Adieu told him while grabbing his hand and dragging him along with her into the town of Kahoy. As they entered she was greeted by bright lights and loud music and very happy people that could barely stand on their own two feet. There were a few women that tripped over themselves and one of them asked Sai if he wanted to have some fun with her.

Though Adieu really had no idea what was going on she saw the discussion in Sai's eyes as he told her no. "Markes where is this hotel so I can get her out of this sinful place?" Sai asked after dodging a man puking on the walkway. "We are almost there, though you may want to hold your tongue. These people may live in the sin of men however it also a holiday today and it is they are festival of the god Greed." Markes told him. "Wait I thought there was only one god?" Adieu could not help but call out a little too loudly. "Child There are so many religions with their own Gods and Goddesses. To be quite honest everyone believes they have it right in some matter of form. Though no one really knows for sure what the truth really is. If I were you I would just believe what you want to believe and don't let anyone else tell you otherwise," Markes told her. "You are known as a Father, should you be really telling everyone that?" Sai asked him. "You forget I am called the Dark Exorcist for a reason. For my, God is the Darkness." Markes told him.

"Then what is my father's name?" Adieu asked with a bit of excitement. "Fang of courses, though I will let him tell you why it's his name himself," Markes told her. "Oh, ok," she told him a little gloom. "Don't worry we will get you back to him," Sai told her. "I know, I just hope he is ok," she told him. "Ok, so when we get to the Cloud inn please for all that is holey stay in your rooms tonight," Markes told them. "Why?" Adieu asked while looking up at every stone building. She was so used to the muddy brick buildings with wooden roofs. "Due to the festival things can become dangerous and I don't have the time to be looking for you two while making sure these drunken fools have not peeled off any of the charms and seals that protect them," Markes told them. "No complaints here," Sai told him though Adieu said nothing for she wanted to look around the new town. She was going so slow that Sai had to grab her hand and drag her along. She was so amazed to see all the decor and all the people in their gid-ups. While being dragged around Adieu saw a small building and there was a wooden sign that she did not know what it said but it had a certain energy that was beckoning her over.

"Markes, what is that building over there?" she asked as she pointed to it. "Markes looked quickly and then right at her, "Can you not read kid?" Markes asked her. "Not real good no," she told him. "It is Kohoy's spice and herb shop," Markes told her while continuing to walk forward. It did not take long after that they arrived at the Inn. "Oh Sir Markes it is nice to see you once again, I have your room all set for you. Oh, you have companions with you this time." a woman's voice shot out from behind the desk. "Yes, these two are going to the Iron gate with me. They could be possible Exorcists themselves." Markes told her. "Well then you are in luck we have one more room available. would you like them together or would you like the young girl to have a room to herself?" she asked. "The boy can stay with me in my room, but make sure this girl gets whatever she needs including food please," Markes informs her. "As you wish Markes, please follow me and don't worry about payment I still owe you for that one job." the woman told him. This woman wore an odd type of dress attire but Adieu liked the design of it.

Adieu followed the woman and could not help but be fascinated by the design on the back of her dress. "That is known as a Cheongsam and the design is a charm that was written in the old language called Asterisk," Markes told her, and the woman just laughed. "Yes, but we don't know how long ago it was used," the woman told them. "Ma'am, may I ask your name?" Adieu asked her, yes, my name is Milly Chan." the woman told her. "This is your room little miss, and your room is two doors further to your left," she told them. "Thank you, it is unorthodox but please come in so I can show you how to work things," Milly told them. When she opened the door it was pitch black in the room though it turned bright in an instant when she flicked a switch. "This switch here turns on your light and the switch next to it turns on the fan in this room," Milly told them and then walked to another room in that room. "This is the bathroom and it works the same way, now the only difference is there is no fan in this room, only heat. Don't hit that switch the hot water will not turn on," Milly informed them.

"If you need anything, this is your room number and all you do is dial 33 and let us know what you need. now since you are with Father Markes your room and food are free, though anything else there will be payment required." Milly told them. "Just let me sleep and that's all I want," Sai told her. "You at least need food for energy tomorrow," Adieu told him while looking at the room. there was a huge bed that had red and gold cloth on it, the carpet was black with silver threads through it, the chair was black and red with wooden features, and the table was all wood. It was so beautiful and she wanted to set on it but she did not want to get it dirty. She went to the other room and saw a giant bathtub buried into the ground, on the right was a place to buy clothing, and on the left had what looked to be a basin and a stool. "Now please wash all dirt off your body before using the hot tub," Milly told them.

"We will have food for you within a few hours, and that will be placed on the table. Now is there anything that you two can not have?" Milly asked them and both of them shook their heads. "Alright then, I shall take you to your room Sir and then you can do whatever you two want," Milly told them. "I have a problem," Aduie announced and both of them turned around and looked at her. "I don't have any clothing," Audie told her and Sai placed his left hand on his forehead. "That's right you're second pare of clothing got burned up," Sai sighed out. "Is there a clothing shop close by?" Sai asked Milly. "Don't worry my dear I will have one of the women bring you clothing, Black correct?" Milly asked. "Yes ma'am," Adieu told her. "Alright then go ahead and get your bath and we will have those clothes here in a few minutes," Milly told her and with that, the two left the room and she was left alone. The room was too big for one person though she was still amazed it was all hers for a night.

She entered the bathroom and saw a basket for clothing and a basket with soaps and bath salts with some sort of not with a smiley face. She took the bar of soap and the bottles and took them to the washing area, and then walked back and turned on the heating system and then undressed. She walked back to the wash area and started the water. The heat of the water flowing over her shoulders turned black with dirt and grim. Her muscles started to become loose after three more minutes of letting the water just run over her. She had to wash seven times before there was no more dirt showing in the water when she rinsed off and she used the whole bottle of shampoo and conditioner before it felt slightly alive again.

There was a knock on the door and when she looked she saw a young girl standing in the doorway of the bath looking at her. "I'm sorry my name is Lyn and I was asked to bring you clothing and see if you needed help washing your back." the girl told her. "I could use some help with my back yes," Adieu told her with a smile.

It did not take long for the young girl to get her back clean and then leave. Though before she did she dumped a pink into the hot tub. Adieu went into the hot tub and sat in for a few minutes before getting out and drying off. She then got dressed in the black slip for bed and headed out the door and into the bedroom. There she saw two sets of clothing on her bed with another note though she could not read it. When she took the close to give to Sai she noticed there was also a silver bag with handles also with a note. She opened the bag and found enough room for her clothing and a new ribbon that had a chain on it. There was a knock on the door and she opened it and Sai was standing there. "Kid that is not an outfit to answer the door with," he told her while rushing her into the room and closing the door behind her. "For the time being, put this on," he told her while throwing her a long robe and she quickly put it on. When she looked back Sai's face was red. "What's wrong with you?" Adieu asked while touching his forehead.

"Never mind me, I came to see if you have gotten your food yet," he told her. "No, but I had a bath," she told him and he just laughed. "Something is different about you," Adieu told him. "Well, I did shave and had a bath too," Sai told her while laughing. "Oh you can read right?" she quickly asked while handing him the notes she found all over the place. "Yes, you can't?" Sai asked, kind of shocked. "No, no one would teach me," she told him. "Ok, let's see this one is from the bath and it says we hope you have a relaxing bath. This one says thank you for waiting and let us know if these do not fit so we can change them to something that does. This is your room number and then has the number to reach the desk. and this one is I noted you had no bag to carry your stuff in please except this and the ribbon inside it for your charm." Sai informed her. "Wow yeah, I guess you do need to replace that. Here give it to me and I will change it to the new one so you don't lose it." Sai told her.

Once Sai fixed her ribbon he put it on her neck, "Hi what do you know it still covers the teeth marks." Sai told her with a smile. "Now try on those clothes and then we will grab a bite to eat," Sai told her. "I thought we were told to stay in the inn?" Adieu told him. "Yeah well Markes is not the boss of us and you wanted to check out that shop didn't you?"Sai asked her and all she could do was smile. "Alrighty then go get changed," Sai told her, and she grabbed her clothing and went to take off the one she had on. "Hold it, change in the bathroom. Do not ever change in front of a male no matter who they are. You need to keep your dignity," Sai told her and she just looked at him so confused. "You are 12 right?" Sai asked her, "I think so according to the village it's been twelve years since I had been there." Adieu told him. "Wait, you been by yourself since you were one? No, that can't be right. Any way we can get that checked no get ready," Sai told her and she hurried to the bathroom and changed.

"Are you ready yet or do you need help changing to?" Sai asked, a bit annoyed. "I'm good I think," Adieu told him. "Good now please stay by my side alright," he told her while opening the door for her. She grabbed the back of his shirt so she would not get separated from him. "Sir, sorry about your food I will have the cook make something for you quickly," she heard Missy's voice call out. "Don't worry about food, though can you have him make some late-night snacks? I will be willing to pay for them. Just for her though I will be going to bed after we come back." Sai told her. "Of course, no payment needed food is free as long as you stay with us," Missy told them. After that, they left the Inn and headed down the pebbled street. "Where are we going first?" Adieu asked him. "Somewhere to eat I think," Sai told her while looking around.

"Also I figured it would be a good chance to teach you some stuff. " Sai told her. "So tell me what buildings are you allowed in?" Sai asked her. "Inns, and caves," Adieu told him. "You are going to be an easy one to manipulate aren't you?" Sai asked her and she just gave him a look. "Lucky for you I amB not one that will do that to you. Now you see that building there?" Sai asked while pointing to a building with people coming out drunk. "Where do people go to get sick?" Adieu asked after seeing someone throw up. "You are half right, but no that is known as a bar, unless you are at the drinking age you do not ever go in there. Each village has an age group that is allowed into the bar." Sai told her. "Are you old enough?" she asked him. "I don't know but with you here I am not asking," Sai told her.

"Well, then what buildings can I go in?" She asked him. "I will show you little at a time," Sai told her while they continued to walk. Pretty soon they came to the store that still pulled her towards it. "This is a spice and herbal shop," Sai told her. They walked in and there standing to greet them was a young woman. "Hello, what can I help you with?" she asked. "My sister wanted to check this place out," Sai told her and moved Adieu to the front of him. "Oh, and what kind of things are you looking for?" the young lady asked while smiling. "Purity," Adieu told her and both the young lady and Sai just looked at her. "Maybe you should explain what you mean," Sai whispered to her. "Oh, I am looking for things that are able to repel demons," Adieu told her and the girl's face went from a smile to a forced smile. "Oh, well I don't know if we have anything for that," she told her. "Oh, well I will just look around then," Adieu told her and started looking at every jar that was on the shelves. "What is this white stuff?" Adieu asked.

"That is salt from the old seas that used to be around here," the young woman told her. "They say that it's the purest substance that purifies water," the young woman told her. "How much?" Adieu asked. "50 Gallons," the young woman told her. Adieu looked at Sai and he let out a sigh, "I am going to have to teach you shopping to ain't I?" "I'm sorry for being a pain," Adieu told him and turned around to look for some more things. "Those are books, they won't help you unless you learn to read," Sai told her. "How about healing herbs?" Adieu asked. "Yes, we have some herbs that can help with healing. We have Genko leaves that help with inflammation and broken bones and Turmeric helps with pain in joints," the young woman told her. "How much are they?" "50 copper each, and that is per a teaspoon." the young woman told her. "So how much for a once then of each?" Sai asked, "3 Gold," the woman told him, "We will take one ounce of each of those and that book on herbal meds." Sai told her.

"That will be 10 gold," the young woman told him and he handed her the money. "Thank you for your business is there anything else I can help you with. "How much for a cup of salt?" Sai asked before leaving the store. "That would be 60 Gold, I would sell it for cheaper if i could but my father chose the prices for today." the young woman told him. "All good, thank you for understanding, I am trying to teach her as many things as I can," he told her and she just smiled. "There is a book store in Hale's that can help her to read," the young lady told him. "Not sure if that is in our travels this time, but thank you," Sai told her and then took Adieu's hand and they walked out.

They walked only to a short distance before coming to a food stand. "Wow that smells good old man," Sai called out. "Uh you are new to town," the old man announced. "Yes, we are only here for the night," Sai told him. "So what shall it be?" the old man asked. "Well I would like some noodles, what would you like Adieu?" Sai asked her. "Anything is good," she told him. "She will have the same but please don't make it too spicy for her. We have to travel in the morning," Sai told him and the old man laughed. "Don't worry I don't make spicy food during the night. It can cause bad dreams." the old man told him as he placed a bowl of noodles in a broth down in front of them. "This is called udon and it is really good," he told Adieu as he grabbed his spoon and tried the broth. She mimicked him with every move until she was comfortable to just eat. "You know this is my last shift tonight. How about some vegetables and some fruit?" the old man asked.

"Sounds good old man but I only have enough for these noodles I think," Sai told him. "What if I help with the dishes?" Adieu asked the old man. "Well if you would like little lady, though there is a lot and you two do need your rest." the old man told her. "Well, then why don't I help as well, after all, if you are closing by yourself it would be too much work for you and I am sure you have to get ready for tomorrow," Sai told him. "That would be nice, thank you. If you are going to do that then all this food is on the house tonight," the old man told them and everyone just smiled. The old man brought out brown crispy things in a bowl for both of them and explained that it was called tempura to Adieu.

After they were done eating that Aduie could not eat another bite. They talked for a few minutes while their food digested, and then got to work. Sai washed the dishes while Adieu dried them and put them on the counter for the old man to put away. They then helped him sweep up the trash around his shop and wash the bar table. It did not take too long and before they left the old man gave Adieu some fruit for their trip. Sai quickly got them back to the Inn and told the lady not to tell Markes that they left the building. Milly agreed and handed Adieu some rice crackers and other sweets for her to snack in a wooden covered box that was red and had gold leaves. "Go ahead and keep that, a girl needs at least a few nice things in her life," Milly told her. "Adieu thanked her and they went to their rooms where Adieu left the box on the table next to her bag and crawled into the bed. Just like Markes told them it was like she was sleeping on nothing.

CHAPTER FIFTEEN
The Food Stall

When the next day came she heard a knock at the door but she had a hard time getting out of bed. Adieu felt as if something heavy was on her body and she could hardly say anything due to the pressure. "Adieu, I'm coming in hope your descent!" Sai called out to her. She heard the door open and then Sai's angry voice yelling out something that she did not quite catch and then the Weight disappeared so quickly. She heard something break and someone trying to plead for forgiveness. She managed to roll onto her back and up at the ceiling, slowly the air went back into her to the point that she was able to set back up and see a man being held to the ground. "What do you think was going to happen, come in here and do what to my sister?" Sai yelled out. "What is going on in... What the hell?" Markes's voice asked as he looked at Sai with the frightened man on the ground.

"I didn't mean to, I thought this was my room. The doors don't lock!" the man tried to explain. "Why should I believe you?" Sai asked him. "Are you hurt?" Markes asked her and it took a moment for her to process what was going on and where she was. "Yeah I think so, What's going on?" she asked while looking at Markes. "Did he touch you?" Markes asked as if he did not hear her. "I don't think so, though my body felt really heavy for a moment," she told him. "Do you feel anything?" Markes asked and she just looked at him. "Like what?" she asked. "Pain anywhere?" Markes asked, "No I feel fine." Adieu told him. "Sai, get off the man, the authorities can take care of him," Markes told him. "Who is that guy?" Adieu asked.

"Just one unlucky man, are you sure you are ok?" Markes asked her as she climbed out of bed.

"Yeah though I could go with some food," She told him. "OK we will get you some food but first go get changed and leave the undergarment in the basket for the authorities to take with them," Markes told her. She had no idea why but she did what she was told, and when she came back out she saw Sai and Markes had tied the man up to the chair. They then met Milly at the desk and told her what happened and to put locks on the doors. She was very sorry that it had happened and looked right at Adieu with pity and she did not understand why she felt ok.

After all the talking both men filled out a piece of paper and then gave it to Milly to give to the authorities. Then all three of them were on their way to the Iron gates again, after they stopped at the old man's shop again. "Ah welcome what would you like this morning?" your special Old Man thank you very much," Sai told him and the man just laughed. "And what about you kiddo?" the man asked her. "Surprise me," she told him with a huge smile on her face. "You got it, and how about you Markes," he asked him. "I will have the rice porridge and salted fish please," Markes told him. "Coming right up," the old man told them and gave a small wink toward Adieu. "So you off to the Irongate again?" the old man asked Markes. "Yes, these two wish to go as well so I am escorting them," Markes told him. "I see, well then young Exorcists please make sure to stop by again within your travels." the old man told them.

"Orkason your place looks so clean this morning. normally after the festival, there is trash everywhere." Markes pointed out. "Oh yes, I had some help last night from some wonderful kids. They did not have a lot of money so they asked if they could work for their food." the old man told him. "Well, you have always been so kind to people, though I am glad to hear they did not ditch on their bill," Markes told him. After a while their food came out and they started to eat but this time he gave Adieu a fork and spoon instead of chopsticks. "May I ask what this is?" Adieu asked the old man and he just smiled. "This is called steam dumpling with a side of rice porridge with some pickled cucumbers and carrots," the old man told her. "If I remember correctly it takes two days to get to the gate from here. Is that right MArkes?" the old man asked him. "Yes thankfully there is a town that is another town close by," Markes told him.

"Would you like some snacks for your trip, with two youngsters you may need your energy." the old man told him and they both laughed. "I am not the one who will need it that is for sure," Markes told him. "You may be right, safe journey Dark Exorcist." the man told him after they were done with their food. "I have one more stop before we leave here," Markes told them. "Alright," Sai told him and once again the Old man gave Adieu food for the journey and gave her a finger to the mouth and whispered. "Don't tell anyone."

"Wow kid, he really likes you," Sai told her while they followed Markes to another shop. "Please wait out here. Also, she reminds him of his own daughter that died at such a young age." Markes told him. "We will wait right here," Adieu told him and watched him walk into the building. They did not have to wait long for within two minutes he was back out and on their way out the Kahoy marble gate. "Now we can't make too many stops, but please let me know before you stop in your tracks. or if you are starting to feel sick, this is going to be a very hot day out here and heatstroke is a normal cause of death out here," Markes warned them. They all agreed and went on their way, "You know I looked out my window and I did not see any comets," Sai pointed out. "That's because it is within two nights," Markes told him. "Two more nights, I wonder if that means they will become stronger too," Adieu spat out. "Are you talking about demons? to my knowledge, they are only strong during the full moon." Markes told her.

"But in two nights it will be a full moon," Adieu pointed out and she heard Markes sigh. "I'm just lucky I just hope nothing gets in our way to enter the gate before that happens," Markes announced. "Well, luck has never really been on my side for long," Sai announced. All became quiet once again as they walked a straight line. "Markes, I have to ask why are you wearing black in a dessert?" Sai asked. "Black is a void color, that goes with any color, though they are the ones that fight the darkness so to blend in they wear it," Adieu spoke up and Markes stopped for a moment. "Who told you that?" he asked her. "I don't remember but that's what I have heard from many travelers within the village of Virgoous," Adieu told him. "Well, whoever told you that knew their stuff," Markes told her. "Wow, that's awesome. so what else do you know kid?" Sai asked. "Not sure, just random things I guess," Adieu told him. "Well, either way, random stuff is better than nothing," Markes told her.

The rest of the journey was quiet for the most part after that, Though at times both men would give Adieu some more random knowledge just to make sure everyone was there. They stopped at least three times before noon time for water, which Markes pulled out canteens from his own bag. "Now make sure you don't drink too much, this has to last you until we get to the next village," Markes warned them. Sai rolled his eyes for he already knew how to live out in the desert. Adieu took a couple of gulps and handed it back to Markes who told her to take one more swig. She did what she was told and then once again handed it back, she then pulled out one of the fruits the old man gave her for each of them. They took them without complaint and ate them on the way. "You know it's not normal to bring fruit into the dessert," Sai announced. "It's due to the fact that it is perishable and the food can ruin them a lot faster. Though Adieu's bag keeps them cool. I asked Milly if she would be willing to find her a bag that would do that for her and one that was fireproof too." Markes told them.

"Now if they could do that with clothing," Sai called out while looking back at Adieu. "Yes, well there are sprays that can help with that. The only thing I am not sure about is if it will keep her from using the fire." Markes pointed out. "That is true," Sai agreed. "is it really that bad for me not to use it?" adieu asked while munching on her fruit. "Yes, because a build-up of your power could kill you. Also, you don't want to lose control over it and hurt those you want to protect. " Sai told her. "How's your pair?" Markes asked randomly. "It is good, I see you finished your apple already, What do you think about your plum?" Sai asked her. "It is good," she told them. "Careful that it has a pit in it you don't want to swallow it," Markes told her. "Why is it poisonous?" Adieu asked. "I don't think so, but you don't want to choke on it either," Markes told her.

It took them until sunset to get to the Next village and this time the Gate was made out of silver. "OH hi, Markes, I see you are not alone today." one of the guards at the gate announced. "Oh hello, Mich how are you tonight?" Markes asked. "All good, just set up the town for the Fiery rain that's coming our way. "Yes, tomorrow night correct?" Markes asked him. "Yes, Sir. How long are you going to be here this time?" Mich asked. "Not long just going to get some sleep and then head straight out tomorrow. I have to deliver these to the Iron Gates before the Fire rain. Everyone should be in the village tomorrow. There is a good chance that Demons will be multiplying tomorrow as well." Markes warned the guard. "Yes, the leader of the village thought the same thing. Well then get on in here before things go bump in the night," Mich told them. They entered the village with the guard followed them. "Welcome to Hakata, now please be on your best behavior," Mich told them as he closed the gates behind them.

"No this place has a red side of town please don't enter that part of town for any reason," Markes told them. "OK, I am not going to ask, "Sai told him and took Adieus's hand so she wouldn't get lost. "Let's just get to the inn and sleep," Adieu told them. Her body started getting really hot and heavy. "Hi, you ok?" Sai asked her and placed his hand on her forehead. "hell why did you not tell us you were not feeling well?" he asked while picking her up. "Where is the infirmary?" Sai asked Markes. "They would not be able to help her, her power is growing due to the fire rain that will be happening tomorrow night," Markes told him. "Then what do we do?" Sai asked him. "We just need to get her body to cool down before she overheats. Come we need to get to the Inn now." Markes told him. "Like putting her in ice?" Sai asked while following him. "Not quite," Markes told him. It did not take long to get to the Inn and Markes barking orders to the Innkeeper and his wife.

They tried everything from lukewarm water to an Ice bath as Sai suggested but nothing worked. "We are just making things worse, what the fuck do we do?" Sai asked. "I don't know every cooling adjacent that would work is not working." Makes told him. "I have a crazy idea, it will either help her or kill her," Sai told him. There was silence for a moment and then

Adieu heard flowing water. "This water is not getting hot," Markes told him. "Go get the manager no!" Sai yelled out. "Hold on kid," Sai told her. The only thing Aduie could hear was her heartbeat racing and her heavy breathing for the longest time. "WE have trouble. The hot water tank is broken and it won't be fixed until tomorrow," Markes yelled out. "Great is there a hot spring or something we can use?" Sai asked. "The only hot spring is in the red distracted," Markes told him. "Then we are going," Sai yelled out while pulling her out of the water.

"It is not like we have a choice though I wish we did," Markes told him. Adieu could hear both huffing and puffing as they walked. She hated the fact that she caused them so much trouble. "We need the hottest bath you have and you need to clear everyone from it!" Markes ordered. This time she heard their footsteps running like something bad was chasing them and then felt something swarm over her. It was so cold and yet Sai's arms never left her body. "Come on kid this is our last resort," Sai told her. "Sai if you stay in there too long you're going to pass out!" Markes yelled at him. "I am not leaving her," Sai told him. "Kid it is not going to do us any good if you both are like she is," Markes yelled. "I don't care! She has a family I do not," Sai told him. "But you are her family to do you not see that?" Markes told him which Adieu wanted to tell him not to be stupid.

When Adieu woke up she felt normal again and when she looked around she saw a room and Markes sitting in the middle of two beds. "Is Sai all right?" Audie asked him. "He overheated himself but he is alright, Though the stupid fool overdid it," Markes told her. "What do you mean?" she asked him. "Well after getting you into the hot spring the water began to boil and as soon as it stopped he passed out. Though he was unharmed, I think it was just the stress that did it to him." Markes told her. "Are we going to make it before the Fire rain?" Adieu asked him. "It's still the same night and it only took four hours to try to get your body to cool down," Markes told her. "Sorry for the trouble, I had no idea anything was happening," she told him.

"It does happen, I should have been warrier about the temperature and your powers. I am just not used to looking after a kid that's a girl," Markes told her. "Well, I guess we are more different than boys than I thought," she said. "No, just a certain thing, yes, I was being careless and I am not afraid to admit that," Markes told her. "So what now?" she asked him, "Now we get you to the IronGate before the Fire rains down on us," MArkes told her. "What happens if they won't accept me?" she asked. "Then I will bring you back to any of these towns and get you a better life than the one you had at Virgoous," Markes told her. "What about Fang?" she asked. "I will personally see that he knows where you are, and I am sure that Sai will stay with you until he does. After all, he cares about you like a sister that everyone could tell." Markes told her.

"Now get your rest and we will continue tomorrow, I already have precautions taken care of in case tomorrow is very hot," Markes told her. "Yes Sir," Adieu told him and then reclosed her eyes and fell back to sleep. When she woke back up she was not in a bed but on Sai's back being carried with a sheet over her. "It is cold," she told him. "I know but we need to keep you from getting too hot again," Sai told her. "How are you feeling?" she asked. "I'm OK, don't worry about me," he told her. "Not going to happen, your family to me I am going to worry about you," Adieu told him. Sai was quiet for a while as they walked, "You are too, that's why I told you not to worry." Sai told her. "Ok we are going to stop here for a moment, let's get some water and food into our bellies," Markes announced. They sat down to eat some dried meat and bread, and then Adieu handed them the rest of the fruit that was in her bag. "Hi, kid what's in that box?" Markes asked as she stuffed it back in the bag.

"Milly gave me snacks, I don't know what kind but I figured our next break we could have them," she told him. "Milly and her snack box are always meant for that person only," Markes told her with a smile. "Keep them for yourself, I have plenty of food to distribute amongst us," he told them. "All right then, but I don't mind," Adieu told them and they just smiled. After that, they packed up and were ready to go, this time Markes carried her until they stopped again. "It is getting very hot how much longer till we get there?" Sai asked him. "A few more hours that's for sure. Though we are almost there, now drink up and eat up. "For now it's been scary peaceful but that can change any moment," Markes told them. "Well I have not used my barrier yet so I think we will be good," Sai told him and Markes just shook his head. "I hope so Sai," Adieu told him while looking to the middle. She felt uneasy when she spotted a dark cloud forming in the desert.

CHAPTER SIXTEEN
Black Flames

"Something wrong?" Sai asked while looking where she was staring and then at her. "I think so, is it normal for the dessert to have dark spots?" Adieu asked both men. "It is normal for hallucinations and mirages," Markes told her. "Let's hope it's all I am seeing," Aduie told them as they finished eating and packed their bag up. By the time they got to the iron gate, it was only midday and everyone was tired. "Markes welcome home, who are these people?" a man greeted them. "Well hello Michael, these two are with me. This is Sai and Adieu, and they are here to meet Father Fang." Markes told him. "The boy can come in, but the girl can't step foot in this place and you know it," Michael told him. "She is Fang's daughter, he told her to come here and by rights, she is honoring her father's wish," Markes told him.

"I didn't know that Fang had a child," Michael told him and his face had a total surprise. "He adopted her, the one man that can always find a loophole in everything," Markes told him. "I'm sorry Rules are rules. However, I can keep her in the hut with me while you try to talk the Elder into it." Michael told him. Markes then looked at Sai and Adieu, "I will do my best guys." Adieu just smiled and then hugged him. "Thanks for at least getting us this far. If you can't get him to do it please don't feel too bad," she told him. "If I can't I will be right out and do what I told you I would," Markes told her. "Sai keep her safe, I will be right out one way or another," Markes told him. "Good luck," Sai told him and then shook his hand.

Both Sai and Adieu waited for Markes in the hobble of a guard post. Adieu just kept an eye on the never-ending growth of darkness heading their way. "Sai are you sure you can't see that?" She asked him. "I really don't see anything, though I do have a terrible feeling something bad is about to happen. Though I am really hoping that I am just being paranoid." Sai told her. "Paranoid?" Adieu asked. "Oh right, um let me see if I can describe it," Sai told her and was silent for a few minutes. "It is a strange feeling that something is about to happen even though it is peaceful around you," Sai told her. "I see, what if you don't see peace and don't feel it?" Adieu asked. "That means you are getting yourself prepared," Sai told her. *I wonder what I am the only one that sees it.*she thought to herself. "You kids doing alright?" Micheal asked them. "Yeah, do you have a telescope that I could use for a moment?" Sai asked him.

"Sure, we have one on the gate ruff," Micheal told him. "Adieu, wait right in here while I go check out the area you are looking at. I will be right back." Sai told her. "Alright," Adieu told him, not even turning her head to him. it only took a few moments she started hearing a voice calling her name but no one was around. After a while, it started telling her to get ready and all she could do was look around. "Holy Shit!" She heard his voice yell out. "So I am not just seeing things," she said to herself. "Adieu! there is a shit tune of demons over there," Sai told her in a heavy breath. "So that's what I have been seeing, but why just me?" she asked. "I don't know but there is a bunch," Sai told her. "Then you better tell Micheal that they are coming and warn the village, judging by the size they will be here by nightfall within the Fire rain," Adieu told him. "He already is letting the village now," Sai told her. "Do yourself a favor, those snacks that you were carrying eat some, your power is going to bring you down fast if you fight hunger," Sai told her.

"I give them to sunset," Adieu told him while handing him some of her snacks. "Thankfully the Fire rain we can use to our advantage if we live that long," Sai told her. "Is that because I have some control over flames?" Adieu asked him. "Yes, do to that fact and with my power of the wind. I can make it to where the flames connect to my wind and use it." Sai told her. "Sounds cool, and dangerous at the same time," Adieu told him and he just laughed. "Just hope Fang is not caught in that," Adieu told him while looking back at the heavy army of demons. "I am sure that he will be alright, I just hope no innocents are caught up in that," Sai told her. "I hope whatever god that is real keeps everyone safe," Adieu told him. "Amen to that kid," Markes's voice came from them behind them. "What's the verdict?" Sai asked him. "The Elder said no, and is sticking to it. Though right now it's on hold until we deal with those things out there." Markes told them.

"I brought you two some food, I know you're going to need it. Though do me a favor don't tell them I brought it to you." Markes asked them. "Not sure why, but sure," Sai told him while taking a loaf of bread and splitting it in half for the both of them. "What about him?" Adieu asked. "I have food for myself," Markes told her while pulling out some dried meat. She took a bite of the bread and heard a continuing crunch as she bit down. "What kind of bread is this?" Sai asked. "Lavender and olive oil, it is homemade and fresh," Markes told him. "It is good," Adieu told him. "Yes, while the Olive oil gives it flavor, the Lavender actually is a natural calmer and it helps the nerves before a battle," Markes told her.

Adieu couldn't help but keep staring at the darkness that kept growing to the point that Sai and Markes were able to see it. "You ok kid?" Markes asked her while still eating his piece of meat. "I understand her being scared, this sinister feeling and bloodthirst chill my bones," Sai told him, and by the sound of his voice, she could tell he would freeze before the battle even started. "I am not scared, I am just wondering if you have enough men for all of those. Also, there are so many they are not just going to come after this village. They are going to attack everywhere, which means my village and Fang, the boy and his mother, and family of three are in danger and there is nothing we are going to be able to do about that." Adieu told him. "Most of these villages have protection though with so many they might not last. It could be the end of the world," Markes told them.

"It's not, most will make it you just have to get to the middle," Adieu heard a woman's voice making her look around her and then back to darkness. "Get to the middle he will be there," the woman's voice called out again and this time she looked right at Sai and Markes. "You know you are just a kid, I can take you into that gate and let you stay there until it's done," Markes told her. "Do you have enough time to fix this?" Adieu asked as she pulled out the gold cross from her bag. "You wait until now to ask that?"Sai asked her in a bit of disbelief. "You know what, I think I can Sai I am going to need some help it should only take a few seconds tops the forge is always going," Markes told him. "Alright, but it better be only a few minutes," Sai warned him as he stood up. Markes took her gold cross and both went on their way, she waited about three minutes before she started walking through the sand. She could hear someone yelling for her to come back but she paid no heed.

With every step she took into the dessert the darker the sky became, small drops started falling on her face. She could not help but listen to the woman's voice that was in her head. She had no idea why but the voice sounded familiar to her and comforting. "Just go straight through," the voice told her. Adieu did not ask questions nor did she want to, there was nothing more to her than to protect whoever she could. She had no idea where her courage came from or why it was there in the first place. "Don't be afraid," was the words of the shadow from her boxed home though with all the demons she was seeing it would only be natural for her to fear. Even though she thought about turning around her legs still carried her forward as if they were not her own. "Who are you?" she asked the Woman's voice.

"Someone, that has always had your back from day one of your life," the woman told her. "I don't understand," Adieu told her, "You will soon enough." the woman's voice told her. "If that is true then why wait now to talk to me?" Adieu asked the voice. "You were never in real danger, and there was always someone to help you when you truly needed it." the voice told her. She reached the beginning of the demon army but none made a move as they could see her. She stopped for a second and took a deep breath and she could feel their cold breath on her skin. Streaks of fire started shooting down the darkened sky and hit the sand around her feet. They had no eyes and they were black smoke skin and some had fur. She saw some of them with bones showing and skin dangling with sharp teeth.

"Why are they not moving?" Adieu asked the woman's voice. "It must be him that is keeping you safe," the voice told her. "Who?" she asked the voice, "Just continue walking, you will be safe but do not accept his offer." the voice told her. Adieu walked further inside the cluster of frozen demons and as she got closer to the middle she saw a man dressed in a black suit and a red undershirt and a black tie. As she got closer she noticed his eyes were pure crimson red and he had a devilish smile with white teeth. An odd excitement washed over her body as she saw the man but had no idea why. "Why are you here?" she asked the man. "Oh I know it has been forever but is that the way to greet you father?" the man asked her while slightly laughing and it was the same sinister laugh she could slightly remember her father having.

"No, my mother and father both died by demons," Adieu told him. "Poor child it is true my human flesh that I wore was torn up by demons and because of that I could not come back to this pathetic mudball my father had made." the man told her. "Yes it is true your mother and I shared a moment and at that moment I was happy. Though my father wasn't happy that I was happy. No, the retch decided to take the power to keep demons at bay for a mere second of my dirty human life and killed all that I loved. Only by you were half my blood you lived except one of the demons' teeth embedded into your neck which helps them keep track of you." The man told her. "I don't understand," Adieu told him, confused.

Within a few seconds of this man telling her about the tooth, her neck started to burn that it blurred her vision. "Ah yes, those things can be pesty," the man told her while walking up to her and placing his hand on her neck. The burning stopped and her vision slowly came back and she heard him chuckle. "You have not grown one bet in power and your body is scrawny, these filthy humans couldn't even take care of my daughter." she heard him hiss out and saw black flames resonating from his body. "Some helped," Adieu told him. "Not enough, they even left you outside like a dog! he snarled. "It was not an ordeal to live but I am alive," Adieu told him. "The word is an ordeal, he told her.

"So I have some difficulty saying words to sue me," Adieu told him, and the woman's voice laughed. "You took your mom's attitude, though to tell you the truth she has been a handful these days," he told her. "Mom been with you?" she asked him. "Yes and no, she has been able to come back to this mud ball in her Spirit form not human," he told her and Adieu just stared at him. "To be honest I was hoping that what she said about you was a lie but that night when I found you in that box I wanted to kill the whole town but what better way to get revenge than to take his daughter away from him as a warning," he told her and then started laughing. "You did that? Why would hurt an innocent?" She yelled at him. "She was no innocent, she was the sinning image as her hateful father. they bathed in riches within their sin," he told her.

"Come with me child and you will never be alone and you can get your own revenge on those who have harmed you. I will let those who have helped you live," he told her. "I don't care about revenge, I have nothing to be mad at," Adieu told him, which in her eyes she didn't, she survived it was all pity to her. "I also am no longer alone, I have Sai and Fang," she pointed out to him.

"You rather live with these weaklings instead of your father?" he asked her. "They are not all weak fathers, and they at least have been here for me," she told him and his smile faded and black flames formed around him. "Then I will take them out!" he told her in a fit of rage. "Fuck that," Audie told him as she triggered her power with the fire rain and sent flames through the army of demons and she could hear their screams all around like echos into the night.

She would have collapsed if it was not for someone grabbing her from behind. "I got you, next time you want to run off don't," she heard Sai's voice. "Sorry I couldn't help it," she told him. "So who the hell is that?" Sai asked her. "Sai, meet my father Lucifer," she told him and he just looked at her dumbfounded. "I did tell you that I was the Devil's daughter," she told him while standing herself back up. "I thought that was a metaphor," Sai told herwhile giving her a slight smile. "Well we still have thousands to go, shall we continue, where do you need to rest?" Sai asked. "How much time can you give her by yourself?" Markes asked him. "Well, if it's not the Exorcist of darkness long time no see Old Friend," Lucifer asked him.

"Well it's the devil himself, Lucy it's been so long I thought we agreed that you would not come back to earth," Markes told him. "It took me forever but yes, but you see a father at least has to check on their kids now don't they," Lucifer told him. "Yeah dragging your child down in that pit should never be a parent's wish," Markes told him. "The only wish I have is to destroy everything that the bastard loves as he did to me," Lucifer told him. "What happened to your family was none of these people's faults. You should have known better to bring demons to a realm that is not your own." Markes told him. "It wasn't I who formed those demons, you dust mites did with your hate and greed. He gave you everything and all you humans wanted was more!" he shouted out. "Your right that humans want more than what they need. Though there are those that only want others to be happy even if it means their pain." Adieu told her father.

As she remembered the elderly couple in her town two years ago working themselves in an early grave to help the town. Those were the only two that would give her food at times at night as they went around the town and fixed things secretly. Any time they were caught the town would give them a small amount of food and money and they gave her the food at those times. When she became strong enough they allowed her to help only if it was not in a building. "Some just want to give back to others the kindness that others give them," she told him while thinking about Fang, Sai, and Markes and how they had helped her and made her life a little better.

CHAPTER SEVENTEEN
Purgatory's Gate

"Markes, you know this guy's strengths and weaknesses?" Sai asked him while trying not to be too loud. "Sorry kid but this guy is not like no other," Markes told him while not taking his eyes off of Lucifer. "Great, you two are acting like old friends that I figured that you would know," Sai told him. "I can't say we are friends, but we were never enemies either. We saw eye to eye at times that is about it" Markes told them. "I see so you never fought together?" Sai asked with a sigh. "Nope sorry again," Markes told him with a smirk. "Well, I guess you and I will have to do our best right?" Sai asks Adieu and all she could do was nod her head. She really did not want to fight her real father, but to protect her family she was gathered in she would. "Sai I think it might be time to put up your wind barrier," Adieu told him.

"I'm already on it kiddo," Sai told her with a big smile. "Use the fire around you, it won't do much to your father but it should strengthen that boy's power and yours." the woman's voice told her. "I don't know who you are lady but I will trust you on this one," Adieu told her in a whispering voice. She could feel the Sai's wind blow gently through her and she stuck out her hand and caught one of the fire droplets and flames spun it. "Feel the wind and find an opening," Sai told her quietly as all three kept an eye on the devil. Adieu closed her eyes and felt the wind as closely as she could but could not feel anything. *What am I doing wrong?* she asked herself. "You have to connect to the boy's heart, though you can only do that if you both care about each other." the woman's voice told her and she couldn't help but blush.

"What's wrong Adieu?" Sai asked her, "I can't find a way to connect," she told him. "What are you talking about?" he asked but she couldn't tell him what the voice told him. "All right, why don't you light your fire and I will then try to combine my wind then," Sai told her. "All right let me try," she told him. With that, she held both her hands up and caught droplets of the fire rain and when she placed them together the flames became bigger. Sai then placed his hand over the flame and she could feel the wind swirling around the flames making them stronger. "It's not ready yet and I don't think he is going to wait for us to attack much longer," Sai told her. She looked right at her father and he started laughing to himself. She could not help but be very annoyed at this.

If only I could connect with the fire rain even more. she thought to herself, and with just thinking she felt the wind puls, and the rain became engulfed in flames to the point the flames became fireballs, and with that, the devil started laughing out loud. "Your powers may not have fully awoken but they are amazing. You should join me not fight me," the devil told her. "She will never go with you, and I won't let her go with you in the first place," Sai yelled at him while taking a hold of Adieu's shoulders. "You have no say in what she chooses to insect," the devil hiss at him. Even though Adieu knew her father was right, she was still happy to hear Sai's words. "I'll kill you before you had any chance to do anything," the devil told him as his flames connected with hers. "You will not lay a hand on any of them!" Markes yelled out as he pulled out a silver-handled blade and doused it in water. Adieu watched in slow motion as Markes charged after her father and stabbed him in his side and then was tossed with a backhand swing.

"Damn, Markes you all right?" Sai called out but they did not hear an answer. "Shit what the Fuck do we do?" Sai asked. Adieu without taking her eyes off her father placed her hand on Sai's, "I have no idea, I never fought before." she told him. "To tell you the truth I have never fought either, I have always had my wind barrier," he told her. "Sai if none of us know how to fight then what are we doing here?" Adieu asked her brother. "To be honest I came over here because you ran off, but maybe we could combine our powers to fight?" Sai told her. "Have you done that before?" Adieu asked him. "No, but we won't know unless we try right?" Sai told her.

"Do you have control over the wind? It does not look like it affects him," she pointed out. "Yeah, I still do what you are thinking?" Sai asked her. "Try to blow some of the fire this way, I can't create it," Adieu told him. "Ok, I will do my best," Sai told her while concentrating and instead of blowing it to her, he sent it straight towards her father. Though she somehow grasped a hold of the flames and both of them raised their right hand and concentrated on her father. *Anything you want to tell me that would help would be nice,* she told the voice in her head through the voice did not say anything to her.

Adieu closed her eyes which she knew was stupid to not watch her enemy but it was the only way to block out everything around her. While she concentrated on the flames she could also feel Sai's determination, and fear at the same time, and when she moved a finger and he started calming down slightly. She then felt deep darkness, pain, and loneliness through her father's flames. Around her father, she felt Confusion and rage that scared her and she could not help but feel sorry for him at the same time. Through her own power, she could feel her own confusion and yet a strong well to protect, and there was no malice within it. She had no idea how she was going to protect everyone and not harm her father to the point of death.

Though she really did not know why she wanted to protect the people that ostracized her for so many years of her life. The feeling of betrayal seeped into her heart and wondered if her father was in the right for what he was doing. "Adieu, you need to concentrate!" Sai told her which snapped her out of her own thoughts. "Let it all go child," the woman's voice told her in an earnest voice. With that, all she did was just screamed as loudly as she could. "They may not deserve it, but for those who have helped me I will save them all!" she cried out and the Dessert became engulfed in flames. Her flames grew to the point that she could no longer feel the wind around her, and they canceled out her father's black flames to the point he looked surprised.

Throughout the flames, she could feel more demons and humans alike turning to dust. Though at the same time the flames passed through Sai, and many other people, she even felt the flames go through Fang which pleased her. She also felt the Flames just go through Markes without harming him though his life force was so low to the point he could die soon. She felt her old village and it passed all but the mayor and his wife, and for some reason, the sheriff and the deputy also went up in smoke though she did not know why. She heard her father Laughing and when she opened her eyes his clothing and skin had been burned to almost nothing. "Damn, how the fuck do we beat this guy?" Sai asked while taking deep breaths. Adieu felt light-headed and almost defeated and collapsed into Sai's chest. "You alright?" he asked her but she couldn't really say anything while she took deep breaths. She could feel both of their power dying down into nothing. "I don't know," she announced for both questions. She could feel her skin burning and she couldn't even stand straight. "Wow, my little girl is pissed at the whole world that much?" her father asked as if he was so happy she just killed so many. "God damn he is hurt everywhere and yet he is still acting like nothing even happened," Sai huffed out.

"You two should have known that flames can not kill the devil," a voice spoke from behind them. Sai turned around while holding onto Adieu and they both saw an old man and Micheal standing there. "Then what would kill him?" Sai asked and with those words, Adieu felt her heart sink. "Nothing can kill him, he is immortal," the old man told him. "Wait what?" Sai complained. "It is true that my father is Immortal, but his mortal flesh can be harmed as you can tell," Adieu told him. "Wait what does that mean? Does he take over human skin or something?" Sai asked. "No, he is at least not that barbaric, he makes his own mortal skin to please the human eye," Micheal told him. "I don't want to know how," Sai told them while trying to keep his small barrier around them both.

Adieu didn't want to know either though at the same time it piqued her interest. She looked back at her father and she saw him already putting himself back together with the dead man ash. "Way to go my child you took your own revenge for me," he told her with a grand smile. "Though why did you leave a lot of them alive?" Lucifer asked her. "I didn't try to kill anyone, it just happened," Adieu told him while looking down at the ground. "The people that she killed no longer had the heart or soul as any human. Those humans mise of well have been the demons that turned to dust as well," the elder told him.

It doesn't matter murder is murder, I will be punished for it somehow," she told him and her father started laughing. "What are you talking about there is no punishment for you. You are my daughter after all," he told her in such a joyous voice that made her almost sick. "Then all you have to do is stay alive and repent for all the lives that you have taken tonight," the elder told her. "You children have done enough, the elder and I will take over from here. Please go take care of Markes for us if he is still alive," Micheal told them. Sai then quickly picked up Adieu and walked behind the two men. Both had no idea what they were going to be able to do if they couldn't even take him down, but they looked around for Markes and found him in the east. "Sai, he is still alive but he needs help. We need to get him back to the gate," Adieu told him. Sai did not question how she knew, all he did was rush to the side of the dark exorcist.

"Damn it, there is no time to get him to the gate. He needs medical attention now or he will die," Sai told her. "Then what are we going to do? I don't have healing powers," Adieu told him, afraid for the dark exorcist's life. "Adieu, I need you to get behind me and close your eyes. What I am about to do you can not watch is you will become blind," Sai told her. "Alright, but how am I to make sure you two don't get attacked?" Adieu asked him. "Trust me no demon will be able to come close to us, and humans will be blinded before even before they make it to us. Now what I am about to do will heal him but both of us will be down for a while." Sai told her. "It won't kill you will it?" Adieu asked him while walking behind him and closed her eyes.

She did not want to lose the only person she considered to be a brother. "It shouldn't, though if it does I am sorry. I have only used it once before," he told her. "Alright," Adieu told him though she was not ok with it. She then placed her hand on his back to let him know she was good. "God, let this work," she heard him whisper. It did not take long for the wind to pick up and heat to resonate from his back. She then grabbed ahold of his shirt for she felt as if she would be blown away. Even though her eyes were closed she saw a bright light flare and felt it go through her body.

Her body felt calm and relaxed as if she had not been fighting all that time. She could not help but smile while thinking that's what a child of God would be able to do. "This boy is not a child of God. He is a Nephilim," the woman's voice told her. "He's a what?" Adieu asked her. "He is half-human and half-angle," the Woman told her. Then what am I?" she asked. "You are half Angle and Half Demon," the woman told her. "You can open your eyes now," Sai told her in such a low voice that she almost did not hear him. She opened them and saw both of the men on the ground. She could feel Sai's life force lower than it was before, and Markes had regained his ten times full. "What did you do?" Adieu asked him, almost mad. "It's a strong healing power that I can use. Though it does leave me drained so I have to be careful how many times I use it." Sai informed her. "Sai, you are killing yourself when you use that. All you are doing is transferring your life into others," she told him while kneeling down to him.

"How many years apart have you used it?" she asked him. "It has been about two years since I last used it," he told her. "Then I am going to ask you not to use that power anymore this year," Adieu told him. "You surprise me you know you surprise me by the way you talk, there are days you can't make a sentence, you stutter, you say words so wrong, and then you just spill sentences like that," he told her. "Did you hear me? You are giving your life force to anyone you use it on!" she told him while getting very annoyed and he just laughed. "Will you k.k.knock it off this is no laughing matter. I can tell you the lost years of your life I just can't tell how many," she told him. "You are too serious for a girl," he told her half-joking before his eyes closed. Adieu quickly caught him and laid him next to Markes.

Adieu stood guard over the two men and at the same time she watched the Elder and Micheal fight her father. She could not understand why the man she barely knew as her father would get hurt it would tug at her heart. "Is there any way to stop this?" She asked herself. "You need to put him back in Purgatory," the woman's voice told her. "How?" she asked. "You need to open the gate," the woman's voice told her. "How do I do that?" she asked though the Woman who did not speak. "Go figure, What are those blades they are using?" She asked while watching them closely. "They are angle blades," Markes told her. "You are awake then?" she asked him without taking her eyes off the fight. "Yeah what happened to him?" Markes asked her. "He healed you, and it took a lot out of him," she told him without wanting him to know until later. "Damn are you alright?" he asked her. "More or less," she told him. "You sound pissed," he told her while getting up and checked on Sai.

Adieu didn't answer, "To think the Elder is going all out with Micheal. You two must have shown a lot of skill for those two to act. Though the others should be ashamed of themselves," Markes told her. "By the way, you were close to death just by one hit from my father, I wouldn't be too upset at your brothers. Sai would not have been able to heal all of them and survived it," Adieu told him while not making eye contact. "You may be right, though we took an oath to protect the people of this world until death takes us," he told her. "They would not be able to continue to protect anyone if they are dead," Adieu pointed out to him.

"Why are you so quick to protect people that you don't know, let alone would not be willing to let you keep your promise to Fang?" Markes asked her. "I am just being practical, If they die by my father then no one will be able to protect anyone during the aftermath," she told him and he just laughed. "Any way would you happen to know how to open Purgatory?" she asked him. "Ok, that's random, but yes I do. All you have to do is spill the blood of an Angel and the blood of a demon and mix them both." Markes informed her.

"Do you know how much blood you need?" Adieu asked him. "I really don't know that answer, I kind of figured death. Why are you asking?" Markes asked her. "Just wondering, I need you to take care of Sai for me. Remind him never to use his powers again for me," she told him and then started running towards the fight. Markes tried calling her to stop, but she did not teach him. "What are you planning? Your father won't like this, please rethink this!" the woman's voice started ringing in her head. "I am sorry I am the only one that can open this gate, I have both, and even if it means my death I will protect these people," Adieu told her. "Just don't die," the voice told her, "I can't promise," she told her.

The only regret I will have is not being able to see Fang and thanking him for everything. Also, the pain that I will cause Sai if I do die. she thought to herself. "You are as reckless as your father," the woman told her which made Adieu stop in her tracks. "Tell me how you are," she told the woman. "I am the one who protects you from the distance," the woman told her. "You already told me that, who are you?" Adieu asked her once more. "I told you that the night you were taken away from me, by the people of this world." The woman told her.

"Mom?" Adieu, ask, "Yes, Your father was always kind to me and these people. Though these foolish humans evolved into greedy and selfish beings that created their own demons and blamed your father for them. Your father thought he could control these man-made demons but found out that he could not. Your grandfather entrusted the darkness to your father when he was a full-fledged Angle still in heaven. With the remaining darkness, his father created man to evenly spread the darkness. His brother had also taken in the darkness when he died to help save these worthless specks of dust. Your father was overjoyed to see some fight the darkness within their souls and treated them with respect. Those who did not fight it after death threw them in Purgatory with his brother Gabriel, " her mother told her. "Then how are you a demon if they are the children of the devil?" Adieu asked her mother while starting to run to the fight once more.

"I was born from a human's desire for lust for one another a long time ago. For the fact, I did not harm anyone that did not deserve it your father fell in love with me. We came down here to be with one another and live amongst these humans. You were born and I only had you for five months before the humans came and stole you away from us. Your father finally got you back after five years before the attack on our lives happened. He asked a friend if anything happened to us to take care of you, and the man agreed. The night our carriage was attacked by your father and my mortal bodies became badly destroyed where we had to leave you. As soon as his friend got you he went back on his promise and left you on the street like the village dog. Watching you grow and not being able to help you tore your father's heart and he gave into the darkness even more." the woman told her. "So both of you were there? Why did you not say anything until now?" Adieu asked her.

"I couldn't talk to you until your power grew, and your father tried but could not no matter how many years it was," she told her. "Once your father was able to come back to this world you were in bad shape," her mother told her. "And that's why Father is pissed off now," Adieu asked her just to confirm. "He is more hurt than anything," her mother told her. "To watch him for so many years as anger grew into his heart was tough." her mother told her. "Then all he needs is to calm down." Adieu pointed out. "Yes, and opening the gate he will have time to cool down since he knows you are doing better now." her mother told her. "If I do die while doing this, where would my soul go?" Adieu asked her. "Purgatory, where all souls go until this world, meets its end," her mother told her. "So that means I will be back with you two?" Adieu asked her. "Yes, but please don't it would crush your father knowing that he caused it." her mother told her. "He should have thought of that before trying to end the world now," Adieu told her and then took a deep breath. "But at least he will not be alone," she told her mother and could not help but smile as she got closer to the battle.

"You are not thinking..." her mother started to say and Adieu tuned her out once she reached the battle. She stood only a little ways from it while watching the blades. She tried to figure out the right time to get in front and not get killed before reaching her father. The elder was tossed back to where he was and he stood there, "Child, I told you to get away from this fight, why have you come back?" the Elder asked her. She did not say anything to him; she was fighting the urge to go back. She had mixed emotions about saving these people if it meant her death. Though she did not want her father to stain his hands with any more blood. She took one deep breath and ran towards her father dodging one of the blades but not the one that hit her within the stomach.

Before anyone realized it another hit her left shoulder and the pain was unbearable and she flung herself against her father. "The Fuck Why?" she heard her father cry out and all she could do was just smile at him. She watched as her father grabbed a hold of her and pulled out the knife within her stomach. He tried yelling something at her but she could not make it out with the ringing in her ears.

She lifted her hand and saw blood all over it and looked down and saw it gushing out. Her father took his hand and took her eyes off of it, while another pair of hands went to touch her. She managed to pull away when the earth began to shake and within seconds the gate to Purgatory appeared beside her. She looked at this black gate of death and saw two cloaked figures that appeared through it and they smelled of death. She found the strength to lift herself up and face these creatures and the blood that was still within her turned cold as ice as one put a blade in her face. "As long as I don't have to watch my father die in front of my face again I don't give a damn if I die," she told it as she touched the blade. The reaper then pulled it away and then placed it in a slit in the door and she watched it open. As it opened there were screams and crying from it, skeleton-like hands crawled out of it and tried to grab her and pull her in. A thick smug poured out into the world and she heard a woman yell pull her back before she felt her body being thrown the other way. she felt arms go around her and as soon as one of the reapers went to grab her, Lucifer went in front of her and dragged her in as he screamed something before she blacked out.

"Come on please wake up," she heard Sai's voice calling out to her. She opened her eyes and was blinded by a bright light. Once her eyes adjusted she saw Sai sitting next to her with his head slouched down. It took her a moment to realize that he was asleep, she tried to say hi but nothing came out. So she slowly moved her arm that felt like it was weighted down to the ground. She was able to loop one of her fingers with him without disturbing him, she felt horrible for she saw the pain on his face and it looked like he was crying too. *How the hell am I still alive?" Adieu asked herself and her mother did not pipe in. She actually felt empty when she thought about her and why she was not yelling at her. She did not know how long it was before anyone else came around and when they did they were complaining that Sai was in her room. At one point she heard Markes's voice in the background.

"He is sleeping in there again? Ok, I will put him on the cot." his voice came closer to the door. "You can't blame him, it's been weeks since that battle," she heard him say. She saw a shadow enter the room and then felt Sai being lifted off the bed. She moved her head to watch him get placed on the cot that was next to her bed. "Oh, you are awake, about the time kid you had all of us worried," Markes told her in a whisper. Adieu tried again to say something but nothing came out once again. "You are in the infirmary in the Iron Gate fortress. You have been out for three weeks due to your blood loss." Markes informed her. "The Elder has ordered your treatment, when asked why he told them that one that risks their lives for others deserves the best treatment," Markes told her while checking her temp. "Good your back to normal," he told her with a smile.

Adieu blacked out once more, and when she woke back up Sai was still asleep in his cot but the Elder was sitting on her bed reading some sort of paper. "Markes told me that you started waking up four days ago," the elder told her. "So I am alive?" Adieu asked him. "Yes, Alive and fully healed now," he told her. "You worried your brother there, barely left your side even to eat," he told her while looking at the sleeping boy. "He did not use his power on me did he?" she asked him. "No, he did not. Though he did try it would not work he was too weak for it again." the elder told her. "I told him not to," she scowled at the sleeping boy. "Don't be too mad at him, it's hard to lose one that you care about more than a stranger." the elder told her. "What happened to my father?" she asked him. "Your father went into purgatory, he fought tooth and nail. Though something like a shadow flew out of you and knocked him through the doors. As the doors closed he threatened me that if I let you die when he makes it out again he would kill me." the elder told her while chuckling a bit.

"I see, at least it was not for nothing," she whispered to herself. "No, it was not for nothing, however since your parents are not here I am going to say it. That was stupid and very reckless of you to do that, when Fang gets back I am sure you will hear more from him." the elder told her and all she could do was look at the blanket that covered her and smile. "Now, I have only one question for you. Would you like to live here?" he asked her and she looked up and straight at him in disbelief. "You can not be an Exorcist, but you can train your powers here without hurting anyone that is intent." the elder told her, and when she opened her mouth to say anything he held up his left hand. "You can take classes and learn about the demons that live amongst us and live with Fang and Sai in this building. You won't be able to share a room with any of them, but still, live with them," he told her.

"Who are you?" she asked him and he just gave a gentle smile. "My name is Gabriel, I am Lucifer's older brother of many." He told her. "So that makes you family by blood then?" she asked him wondering where the hell he had been all her life. "Yes, and when I came to get you I was told I would be arrested on the spot and locked in a dungeon if I stepped onto their land. I sent two men to claim you but none of them made it back alive." Gabriel told her knowing full well what she was thinking. "When Markes told me that you were at the gate I did not believe him. So I came to check out the girl that was at my gate and saw the battle with you three.

I knew right then who you were and asked Micheal to come out with me. I told the other men to stay put in case you and your father lost control of your selves." he told her. "Does that mean you are a fallen too?" she asked him as soon as the thought popped into her brain. "No, like Lucifer I wanted to help the people of this world. Though because I did not have the darkness within me I could not help them the way I wanted to. So I formed this place to destroy the demons of men," he told her. "Why did your father put the darkness within my father instead of himself?" she asked him. "Father did put it in himself, but it started taking over his heart. Lucifer most of it from him to the point father was able to make mankind out of sand and darkness," he told her.

It became quiet as she processed everything that he told her. "Will you accept your uncle's offer?" he asked her. "As long as I get to live my life the way I need to, and am not going to be trapped here then yes. However, if I am getting told no I can't leave then sorry I will find a way out of these gates and find my own way in life," she told him. Gabriel smiled at her, "There will be no chains attached and on certain missions, you will be allowed to go with them if you would like." he told her. "Then fine I will stay here and wait for Fang like he asked me to do and then I will see what goes on from there," she told him and then watched him leave the room with a smile on his face. Within a few seconds later Sai entered the room. Once he realized she was awake he rushed to her and threw his arms around her. "Thank God you're alive!" he cried out.

"Sai,cant breath," she told him and he quickly let go. "I have so much to tell you but first I have a letter for you." Sai told her while handing her the letter. "I can't read, remember? And who is it from?" she asked him. "Your father Fang. I can read it to you if you would like." he told her. "Sure," she told him while leaning against the wall behind her. "OK," he told her while opening the white envelope. "It says,

Dear Child,

I hope you found your way to the Iron wall, I was able to get the woman and her boy to safety. Sorry that I am not there with you and sadly to say I wont be with you until after a year. I was called by Our Lord to go to another village and what I have found is going to take me that long. I want you to live your life and let whoever is at the Inn that you are my daughter. They will take care of you until I can get to you.

From Fang

"What does he mean Iron wall? I thought you said Iron gate?" Sai asked her, a bit confused. "I guess I remembered it wrong," Adieu told him, slightly smiling. "Well when you get better we will go to the right place," Sai told her. "I told the Elder that I would stay here," Adieu told him. "Well in a year we can go and make sure you meet him there," Sai told her, slightly confused. "Sounds like a plan," Adieu told him. "What happened after I blacked out?" she asked him. "I don't fully know, I woke up after a scary door went into the ground. Markes won't tell me what happened but he did say you may not make it.

You nearly died on me three different times. I couldn't even heal you. It was like my powers blocked themselves." he told her and she just gave him a scowling look to show she disapproved of him trying. "I still can't use them, so the elder said that I could live here and learn the human way to protect the ones I care about. Of course I told him the only way I would do that is if he allowed you to stay with me." Sai told her. "I guess both of us will be learning those tricks. He told me I could live here, after all he is my uncle," she told him and Sai just smiled. "Great, no matter what I won't leave you." he told her. "Thank you, we will get your power back and then after a year we go get Fang." she told him.

CPSIA information can be obtained
at www.ICGtesting.com
Printed in the USA
BVHW031440080521
606755BV00006B/668